table of contents

Mission
to
Seoul

by
Thomas
Wood

mission to seoul

Green Hills Press
Nashville, Tennessee

© 2012 Thomas Wood

Cataloging-In-Publication Data
Woods, Thomas
Mission to Seoul
ISBN: 9780985534202

BISAC Subject Code: FIC006000
Fiction / Thrillers / Espionage

Distributed by Grave Distractions Publications
www.gravedistractions.com

Printed in the United States

FOR A CAT CALLED GIGI

1

return

Boyce Mann stood on the foredeck of the ferry and watched lights from the port of Pusan, South Korea emerge from the sea before him. He had been waiting to see them for twenty-four hours, since the creaky vessel that brought him from Japan departed the port of Osaka at daybreak the day before for its journey through the Inland Sea from the Land of the Rising Sun to the Land of the Morning Calm. He had not bothered to book a sleeping berth because he knew he would not be able to sleep. He was too excited, too anxious, too frightened to relax and rest, to sleep. His trip back home would demand all of his strength, yet he knew he could not prepare for it by sleeping.

Boyce was tall and trim for a man of almost 46. His colleagues and students at Davidson teased him about looking like a minor, B movie actor, "Cary Grant without hair dye and make up," they said. Even the gray in his hair and the creases in his face were the advantages, not disadvantages, of male aging. He was not particularly careful about exercise and diet, just the inheritor of good genes and metabolism... His suit—pants and jacket of different purchases, shirt slightly frayed about the collar and cuffs, necktie not quite tied to perfection—reflected his lack of concern about appearance. He looked good without really caring or trying.

The April sun was just rising over Japan behind him, dispelling the thick Asian night, offering him sight for the trip he had begun over a week earlier and knew would not end any time soon. He was just able to see the outline of the city, but he could tell that it had been greatly altered by the twenty eight years since he last saw it. The buildings along the coast were taller. He had departed the land of his birth from this city when he was eighteen, and he was returning for the first time at the age of forty five. He did not know how long he would be here. It might be only a day or two, or he might be much longer. He didn't know that it would be forever.

In 1948, with his parents and younger brother Andrew at the dock to see him off, Boyce had taken this same ferry from Pusan to Osaka, then an ocean liner from Japan to California, then a train across the American continent which he had never before seen, to Princeton, New Jersey. Now in 1976 he had flown from Atlanta to San Francisco and then from San Francisco to Osaka. In 1948 the trip had taken him two weeks. This time it had taken less than twenty hours. In 1948 he had left an optimistic Korea, just proclaimed a republic, to pass through a Japan still devastated by the world war only three years finished. In 1976 he found Japan resurrected to prosperity and optimism about the future. He knew from the media and letters that he would find a Korea divided North and South, the South prosperous but pessimistically living under the iron fist of a dictator who reflected the attitudes and practiced the policies of a fascist.

He had kept all the letters that reached him in America over the 28 years he had been away, the ones addressed to him at Princeton University, where he earned three degrees, the ones addressed to him at Davidson College, where he worked his way up to a full professorship. The ones from the first two years were full of hope. The post war partition would soon be over and the Republic of Korea would once more be a united and independent nation, with a democratic government favorable to Christian missions. The two Christian colleges which his grandparents had founded and his parents had given their lives to cultivate, one for boys and one for girls, were growing and flourishing. So was the orphanage his mother had founded. American Presbyterians, now that the United States was recovering economically, were sending ever more generous amounts of money for new buildings and new degree programs. His brother Andy would be able to join him at Princeton in 1952 and do his undergraduate studies there while Boyce finished his seminary training.

Then in January 1950, United States Secretary of State Acheson made his famous statement about American commitments to Asian security and failed, either by accident or by design, to include Korea, leaving the impression that it was outside America's zone of interest and protection. Six months later, the North Korean Communist army crossed what was supposed to be a temporary dividing line at the 38th parallel. The next six months were chaos. After June 1, 1950, Boyce received not a single letter from his family, until the middle of November; and during those months he had to depend on newspapers and radio for information.

He learned from printed articles a week old and radio broadcasts so full of static he could make out only a few scattered sentences that the traditional capital Seoul, where his parents and brother lived and worked, had fallen to the communists.

Every morning he rose before dawn to get the latest transmission: McArthur arrived from Japan in July to lead a United Nations force; that force was pushed all the way south to the Pusan Perimeter in August; McArthur launched a counter attack from the sea at Inchon in September and pushed the enemy north across the 38th parallel, almost to the border of China.

The first letter to reach Boyce since the end of May was dated October 1st and arrived October 15th. His mother was ebullient. The family was all safe, as were the colleges. There were no damages to the buildings and no student or orphan deaths. It had been a terrible four months, but now victory seemed assured. General McArthur was nearing a complete victory in the north, performing the miracle in Korea that he had in Japan, where he had saved the nation and established a democracy. Under his direction Korea would now be united, it would be democratic, it would be Christian. She urged Boyce to pray for the valiant general who had redeemed Japan and now had saved Korea. That was the last letter he received from Korea for a year and the last ever from his mother. On the day that letter reached him in Princeton, a Chinese Communist army of unimaginable size crossed the Yalu River into Korea, responding to the arrival of United Nations forces on the Yalu River, and Korea fell into a paroxysm of bloodshed.

Boyce went to his local draft office and tried to volunteer for the U.S. Army being expanded to counter the invasion. He explained that he was born in Korea, spoke the language like a native, and had family in Seoul. Officials balked. He was physically fit enough to go, they said, but what were his political views? How had his family kept peace with the demonic Japanese during the war? Had he ever had Communist friends? He assured them his family had not supported the Japanese occupiers but had cooperated with them in order to remain in Korea and minister to the Christian community there. He had never known a Communist and did not agree with their atheistic philosophy or their communal economic system. Was he volunteering just to return to see his parents? He wanted to see them, of course, to make sure they were safe, but that was not his only reason for wanting to go. He loved Korea and its people and wanted to help them in their struggle. Would he expect special treatment because he spoke Korean and knew the country? No, he just wanted to go and help save his country from this menace. Was he Korean, or was he American? He was both. How was that possible? He was an American citizen born and raised in Korea. He was told to wait for further word, but it never came. He returned to the office each month, but he was always told to wait. He realized after a time that he was under suspicion and a commodity too hot to handle. He would not be called.

So he fussed and fumed and tried to keep his mind on his studies and waited for letters, but none came. Not at Christmas, not in the new year of 1951. He could barely eat, and he slept fitfully. Finally at close to midnight on a Wednesday in March, as he was undressing for bed, a knock came on his dormitory door. Expecting to see a classmate who regularly came to him for help in his Greek lessons, he was surprised to open to a man dressed in a trench coat. The man flashed a badge and identified himself as an agent of the Central Intelligence Agency. He came into Boyce's room without being invited, and took a seat, also without being invited.

"You're Boyce Mann? Boyce Mann the Third?"

"Yes. Yes, I am," Boyce said uncertainly.

"Born in Seoul, Korea, to missionary parents. Reverend and Mrs. Boyce Mann, Jr."

"That's right. What... "

"Got some bad news for you, son," he man said, taking a cablegram from his coat pocket. "You know of course that Seoul fell to the Communists for the second time in January."

"Yes, sir." Boyce felt his stomach churn.

"Government regrets to tell you that the place where your mother was working... is it an orphanage?"

"That's right."

"Communists broke in, set fire to the place, killed several of the children and adult caretakers, and among the ones they killed was your mother. That would be Mrs. Emily Mann, am I right?"

Boyce dropped his eyes and nodded.

"As I said, we regret it; and I hate to be the one to tell you."

"Thank you."

The man got up, folded the cable and replaced it in his pocket, and left as quickly as he had arrived, disappearing down the darkened hallway, leaving Boyce to his private grief.

Boyce heard no more from his family. He somehow got through the spring semester with passing grades and kept up with the news as President Truman fired General McArthur in April, as truce talks began in June, as a ceasefire went into effect in November, only to be broken over and over again. At last a letter reached him just before Christmas. It was written by Kim Ji-wan.

Kim Ji-wan was a Korean girl who had grown up in his mother's orphanage. She was a bright, happy child, the same age as Boyce. His mother had always wanted a daughter, and she treated Ji-wan as her own. In the letter Ji-wan gave some details, but likely not all she knew, about Emily Mann's death. She said that Boyce's father took his wife's death hard and that his health was fragile. He had dysentery, and there was no medicine to treat him. She was about to take him and Boyce's brother Andy "to the mountain retreat" for rest and safety.

Boyce knew where they were going. It was a remote mountain hideaway that his family had owned for fifty years. A hundred acres on a hillside. They went there regularly during the hot summer months. He hoped they would all be safe. Still he made an effort to go home, not as a soldier but as a son who needed to be with an ailing father. No, he was told at the federal building in New York, negotiations were delicate. The government could take no chances with people who were neither Korean nor American because they were both.

Boyce graduated in the spring of 1952 and was at Princeton Theological Seminary in November when Eisenhower was elected. He was completing that first semester when Ike visited Korea, fulfilling a campaign promise. He was about to enter his second year of seminary training when the permanent cease fire went into effect in the summer of 1953. It was only after the cease fire, when Korea was once again divided along the 38th parallel, that a second letter from Ji-wan reached him. She explained that this was the first time the postal services would take a letter. His father had died at Christmas, 1952. He was just 56 years old.

Boyce wrote back thanking her for the news, bad as it was, and asked her for word of Andy. Now that mail was being processed regularly, he heard from her within the month. Andy was in good health, if not in good spirits. He was adjusting. He asked her to tell Boyce that he would not be coming to America to study. He preferred to remain in Korea. He did not want to learn new ways. He had been hired by an import company and lived alone in his own house. Ji-wan told him that she was assuming the directorship of the orphanage, and she encouraged him to return home as soon as possible.

He wrote back saying that since his parents were gone, he would wait now until he had finished his seminary training and hope the Presbyterians would appoint him to a mission post in Seoul. It would only be two more years.

She wrote that she would be overjoyed to have him return to Seoul. She described the memorial service for his father and mother. Representatives of all the Christian denominations spoke, as did the most revered Buddhist priest, as did President Rhee, as did the King, now without a crown in the republic but still a leading moral figure. His parents' remains had been moved from their original, temporary resting places, hers on the orphanage grounds, his in the mountains, and they were reinterred on Missionary Hill, one of the most sacred spots in Seoul, near the graves of his grandparents.

Boyce laid the letter down on his bed and shed bitter tears. He promised God in his sorrow and loneliness that he would go home as soon as possible. He would take up his family's mission. He would fulfill the promise he had made to Ji-wan that night behind the church altar as American bombs rained down on them during the Japanese withdrawal. He kept none of these promises. Only now, after so many years, was he returning.

Boyce could have flown from Osaka directly to Seoul, but he had purposely lingered in Japan for several days. Visiting Kyoto with its ancient shrines, telling himself that he should soak up some culture. In reality, Boyce was dreading his return to Korea. When he finally knew that he could put it off no longer, when he saw that there was no way further to delay the inevitable trauma of returning to the land of his parents when they were not alive to greet him, he decided to take the ferry over and the train up country to what he still called his home town.

At long last, after a slow entrance into the harbor, the ferry docked, and Boyce came slowly, warily down the ramp with his one suitcase and entered the immigration office. At once he recognized the smell of Korea, the essence of garlic that every Korean exuded because of their diet. He had, when first at Princeton, sought out a Korean grocery so that he could buy and eat kim-chi with his meals; but the ribbing he took from his class mates about his breath made him give up his favorite garnish. He had given up eating any form of Korean food and he had not smelled its pungent odor for over a quarter century.

Neither in that quarter century had he seen so many Korean faces in one place as he saw them now. The soldiers in uniform who stood guard over the entry and exit doors to the processing room, the young women, also in uniform, who questioned arrivers about their purpose in visiting Korea, the young men dressed in blue suits who frisked the men and young women also dressed in blue suits who frisked the women, they all had the distinctive facial features that made Koreans the most handsome yet also the most menacing of Asian people.

The young woman who flipped through his passport and looked up into his eyes to question him spoke perfect English, with the exception that on occasion she omitted articles, as in, "What is purpose of visit to our country?" Boyce answered her in Korean, "to visit my brother, who lives here," and although he had not spoken it for many years he felt he spoke Hangul more correctly than she did English. She was startled by his answer.

"Where you learn to speak our language?" she asked in English.

"I was born in Seoul," he answered in Korean. "I lived there until I was eighteen years old."

"I see," she said. "Please step to side and wait for moment."

He moved over and watched as she got up from her desk and hurried through a door behind it. In a moment she returned and asked him to follow her. Through the door he saw a small, brittle Korean man with a cigarette smoldering in an ash tray before him. The little man beckoned Boyce to sit down at his side.

"You are Boyce Mann?" the little official said in English.

"Yes, I am," replied in Korean

The little man frowned and switched to Korean, which was obviously easier for him. "And you say you were born in Seoul?" He looked down at Boyce's passport, which indicated that Boyce was just a month shy of his forty sixth birthday. "You were born here in... 1930?"

"Yes, that's right."

"Please explain how that could be."

"My parents, and indeed my grandparents before them, were Presbyterian missionaries. I left in 1948 to attend university in America... "

The little man interrupted. "You are... of the Mann family, the famous missionary family, who founded Yun-sei and Ee-wah schools?"

"Yes."

The little man's face broke into a big grin. He stood and offered his hand. Boyce rose and took it. "I am a graduate of Yun-sei," the man said. "It is indeed an honor to meet you. Are you here to visit your brother?"

"Yes," Boyce said, without making any further explanation. His brother was only one reason he had returned—and not the major one. "So you know of my brother, do you?"

"Of course. He is a most respected citizen. Welcome, Mr. Mann. I will not detain you further. Are you returning to live here?"

"No, I have a job in America. I'm just here for a week or so."

"And why didn't you fly directly to Seoul?"

"I wanted to return the way I departed, to retrace my steps. In 1948 I came to Pusan from Seoul on the train, then took the ferry to Osaka. Now I return by the same route."

"Oh, such a good idea. Very, may I say, Confucian." He led Boyce out of his office and personally stamped his passport. He lifted Boyce's suitcase and handed it to him. "Would you like a ride to the train station?"

"No, thanks," Boyce smiled. "I need to walk. Is it still only a short distance from here?"

"Yes. A kilometer at most."

Boyce shook his hand. "Thank you, sir. I'll be on my way then."

He walked past the armed guards at the exit door and out into the waking town. The architecture, the working people on the street, the signs printed in the characters created in the sixteenth century to represent the sounds of the language were all familiar. He clearly remembered that day so long ago when he walked down this same street with his parents and younger brother.

After 1953 the letters from Kim Ji-wan gradually grew less frequent. At the same time Boyce grew less anxious to return home. When he finished his divinity degree in 1955, he entered the Ph.D. program in art history; and by the time he finished it in 1959 he no longer wanted to see Korea again. In graduate school he met and married a southern belle, who reminded him of his mother. She was Mary Lee McGinnis from Savannah Georgia; and she persuaded him to send out resumes to southern universities. In 1960 he was hired by Davidson College, a Presbyterian school in North Carolina, and spent the next decade earning tenure and a full professorship. He and Mary had no children, and she died in 1970.

Regular letters from Ji-wan, which had been few and random for nearly two decades, resumed shortly after Mary died. She knew nothing of Boyce's life in America, but she hoped she could call on him for advice. She could not rely on Andrew. She told him that she was now dean of Ee-wah University for women and that she had used her position to speak out against the oppression of the dictatorial Yi regime, which for a decade had collected and exercised dictatorial powers over the Korean nation. She was considered a trouble maker for the way she had spoken out against the way he had stripped many leading Christians of their human rights and even sent a number of them to prison.

Boyce answered each of her letters, explaining that he knew about circumstances in Korea only from what he read in American newspapers, where Park was considered a valuable anti-communist ally to the U.S. interests in Asia, especially with the war continuing in Vietnam. He urged her to be careful, not to take unnecessary chances, not to run the risk of imprisonment herself. She replied that she felt she was obligated to carry on the work his grandparents and parents had begun in her country and that she could not be silent when her people were suffering.

Boyce applied for and received a Sabbatical leave for the school year 1975-1976; and he left in September for Italy. He felt he needed to see for himself the works of the Italian Renaissance he had been showing and explaining to his students on transparencies. That fall he lived in a small apartment in Florence and spent long days in all its grand museums, with weekend visits to Rome, Venice, Bologna, and Sienna. On one long day he took a train from Florence to Empoli, then a local bus to Vinci, and then walked two miles into the countryside to visit the birthplace of Leonardo. A graduate student at Duke, who was living in his house while he was away, sent his mail at two week intervals, and the letters from Ji-wan continued to be included in the packets until November, when they stopped. In the second March packet came a letter from Korea, but the handwriting was unfamiliar.

The writer introduced herself as Kim Ji-wan's assistant dean. She was distraught to tell him that Ji-wan was in jail. He had surely heard about the attempt to assassinate President Yi, when he was not injured but his wife, the first lady, was killed. A two year investigation and search for the perpetrators had concluded that several Korean Christian leaders were involved in the plot, among them the outspoken critic of the regime Kim Ji-wan. She was arrested and awaited trial. If convicted she could be executed. Please, please Doctor Mann, please come to her aid. Your prestige, your family legacy, Your position as a prominent American college professor, would do much to help save her from this terrible fate. You must come and come as quickly as possible.

Boyce had always felt guilty for not returning to Korea to work, for abandoning his family's mission for the more comfortable life in America. To offer whatever support he could to Ji-wan in her need seemed a small sacrifice to make. So on the night he received the letter of appeal he packed his bags, left Florence in the last day of March, made a transitional visit to Charlotte to check on his house and office before flying out for Japan, all the time reading newspapers for information about the accused assassins. A second letter from the same writer reached him in Charlotte. No definite word on the trial, but come as soon as possible.

On the way to the train station Boyce passed a clump of Korean kids gathered at a street corner. One of them spotted him, his eyes widened, and he nudged the one next to him, who responded with wide eyes and nudges of his own. In a moment the whole group was staring at him. One of them pointed at him and said, "Mikuk saram." It was the Korean word for "Americans," but it was used to identify any white person.

Without slowing his pace, Boyce grinned at the boy. He pointed back at him and said, "Hankuk saram." Korean.

The little boy's mouth fell open, and his hand dropped, but his eyes remained wide. One of the other boys began to laugh, and in a moment they were all laughing. This white man, this American, understood their language and could speak it.

Boyce went on, smiling, knowing he was home again.

2

morning calm

In the Year of Our Lord 1885, thirty years after the Hermit Kingdoms of Japan and Korea were opened to Western trade, three years after the first U.S. Embassy opened in Seoul, the Protestant churches of North America met to discuss plans for the evangelization of Asia. They concluded that instead of competing, duplicating their efforts in the sprawling mission field, they would divide the area up into zones of responsibility. The peninsula of Korea, where the people had for many years been under the influence of the powerful but declining Empire of China, was given to the Presbyterians. In 1887, in a hurry to bring the Gospel of their Lord and Savior Jesus Christ to the sons of Han, the first two Presbyterian missionaries arrived in the Land of the Morning Calm.

Clarence Jackson and Boyce McMann, both of Scots-Irish stock, stood on the deck of the ship that had brought them from Japan and circled the peninsula until it arrived at the Port of

Inchon. They had been classmates at Princeton, seniors in the divinity school, when a chapel speaker announced that the church needed volunteers to be missionaries in Korea. They did not know each other well, but both wanted to be missionaries—Johnson had planned to go to Brazil, McMann to India—and they were both fascinated by the idea of serving the Lord in this new field. They came forward at the end of the sermon to ask the speaker questions; they began meeting between classes to discuss books they were reading on Asia; and they were both highly pleased when word came at graduation that they had been chosen to open the mission to Seoul.

They were both married, but both wives were prepared to follow their husbands "to the ends of the earth," and changing directions from Latin America and India to Asia did not faze them. The two couples met frequently as the men took a crash course in the Korean language and as the women, Wilma McMann and Hazel Jackson, packed for the long journey. They travelled together by train across the continent to San Francisco, where they boarded a freighter to Japan. In Japan they joined the Presbyterian mission community, and the wives remained there while the men went on to Korea. The wives would follow when their husbands thought things were ready for them.

As Jackson and McMann stood looking across the shallow water that separated them from the land of their dreams, the captain of the boat, a crusty, bearded old Yankee sailor, came up to them. "Well, Preachers," he said with a hoarse cough, "it's gonna be a while. We can't land as of yet."

"Why not?" Clarence said. He was anxious to set foot in the country where he had chosen to fulfill his promises to preach the Gospel to all peoples.

"The tide," the skipper said. "It's the damnedest place in the world, second damnedest to Halifax in Nova Scotia, the way it rises and falls so far. I misjudged our speed over from Japan. Thought we'd get here after it rose, but we arrived early, so it ain't up to landing yet. I judge it'll be another three, four goddamn hours before I can set you down on land."

Offended but undeterred by the sailor's language, Boyce spoke up. "So we're stuck, are we? Three, four more hours?"

"Aye."

Boyce looked at Clarence and raised an eyebrow. Clarence returned the look and grinned. They both nodded. The captain was startled when the two men of God suddenly stripped off their shirts and removed their shoes and plunged into the shallow water. He called out to them to watch out for the tricky tide, but they didn't hear him in their mad dash through the water toward the shore. They didn't stop until they had come up on the sandy bank and waved back to the boat.

"Crazy couple a bastards," the captain said to the crew that had gathered to watch the spectacle. "They're gonna get theirselves killed for sure, one way or another, you can bet on it."

On the shore Clarence and Boyce embraced, laughing, and exchanged friendly insults.

"I thought you said you were a prize winning swimmer," Boyce teased Clarence. "Said you had ribbons and medals back in Connecticut. "I beat you easily, and I don't have any prizes."

"You were lucky," Clarence laughed. "You caught me at a bad time. I'm definitely overweight, have too much to carry. Guess I should've pushed back from the table quicker these last few months. Need to lose a few pounds."

"From what I've heard about the food here, that may not take much will power. They say it's hot."

"Well, as soon as I'm back in shape, we'll do this again; and next time you'll swallow the water flying off my feet."

"Ha!"

"Ha!"

They wandered up the bay to the dock, where a Korean man who spoke acceptable English met them. He explained he was from the U.S. Embassy in Seoul and was sent to bring them safely up river to the capital city. As soon as the boat carrying their luggage finally made it to the pier, the man hired local workers to transport their belongings from the ship to a small skiff, and they set off for their new home. By that time they and their clothes were dry.

On the short trip up the river, the two men scanned the banks for first impressions of Korea. On both sides rice fields stretched as far as the eye could see. They were surprised and mildly offended to see Korean women working in the fields and washing clothes in the shallows, all of them bare breasted, and without any sign of embarrassment. The women stood up from their labors and waved at the passing boat, their breasts moving with their arms. The two men noted that the Korean faces were different from those in Japan and from those of the Chinese sailors on their ship across he Pacific. Koreans were more beautiful than other Asians, yet they also bore a fierce look, as if centuries of oppression, both from foreign overlords and their own native rulers, had made them handsome and deadly.

Their guide took them to the U.S. Embassy, enclosed by stone walls, and led them through the heavily guarded gate, around behind the Residence, to a small house which served as guest quarters. He showed them the house, with its two bedrooms and a communal bath, and told them that the ambassador would come for them to have dinner with him at sundown. He left them, and they unpacked the bags which held their clothes. The ones holding their Bibles and other books could wait until they were in their own digs. Boyce bathed first, lingering as long as he thought he had a right to do, in the warm water. Then he drained the tub and started a fresh supply for Clarence. When Clarence had finished bathing, he came out to find Boyce sound asleep. He followed suit, and they both slept soundly until bells from an unknown source woke them. They began to dress for dinner, but before they were fully ready, a knock came on the door. It was the ambassador.

Theodore Blackmond was a tall, slightly stooped, grey haired man, impeccably dressed; and he had the air of someone who does a somewhat unwelcome job because it is his duty to do so. He welcomed them to the Residence and led them on a slow walk around the grounds. The place, he explained, had been the home of a Korean prince who died without heirs, and the government had leased it to the U.S. mission in exchange for special trade rights with their new friends across the Pacific. The Koreans, he explained, were anxious to make allies to protect them from their old predators the Chinese and their new predators the Japanese.

Over a dinner of Australian beef and Idaho potatoes (his served with a fine French wine, which the two missionaries declined and had barley water) he told them of his career in the U.S. Navy, from which he retired two years earlier with the rank of Rear Admiral. He had meant to go home, to Pennsylvania, to a farm he had bought during his years on the high seas; but duty called. President Cleveland asked him to take a turn as the first U.S. ambassador to the Kingdom of Korea. When a president asked this of a man, the man must obey. Now that there was a new president, he didn't know how long he would be continued, but he planned to stay on as long as he was needed.

"How long do you think that will be?" Boyce asked him.

"I hope not long. Perhaps another two years. President Harrison may have another person in mind already. And I don't mind at all. I'm tired. I want to go home again, to be an American."

"We hope you will stay as long as possible," Clarence said.

"Thank you, but I'm not sure that is a friendly wish," the ambassador smiled. "One thing I can say for sure, you two men will be here longer than I am."

The men finished their meal, and a servant brought coffee. The ambassador opened a box and showed his guests a collection of Dutch cigars. They declined his offer, and without asking them if they minded he removed a cigar, set it alight, and began to smoke.

"You two young men seem bright and gifted, and of course well educated since you come from Princeton; and I'm sure you will serve the best interests of your country in this land."

"Well, sir, it is of course Christ that we serve," Boyce said.

"Yes, yes, I know," the ambassador nodded and blew out a mouthful of blue smoke. "But service to Christ and service to the stars and stripes, they are not contradictory missions. I firmly believe that the United States of America was founded to be a light to the nations, to show them the path of democracy and the path of Christianity, the same path, I believe."

"We hope that is true, sir," Clarence said cautiously.

"It is, it is," the ambassador said firmly. "By the way, your names, they are a bit cumbersome for the Koreans. You will have to shorten them."

"Sir?"

"Yes. Koreans are used to short names. I learned very quickly that Theodore Blackmond was too big a huge mouthful for most

Koreans to chew. So I shortened it. I am now called Dore Mond. Makes life a lot easier for all my staff." The two guests smiled. "You must do the same. It's Boyce McMann, am I right?" he asked.

"Yes sir," Boyce said.

"Well the Boyce is all right. It's a bit complicated, but they should be able to get their tongues around it. But McMann is redundant. Lop off the Mac, make it Mann. Just tell them you are Boyce Mann."

Boyce smiled and shrugged. At that moment he thought the idea ridiculous. Within two weeks he saw the wisdom in the old man's advice and followed his suggestion. Thereafter he was Boyce Mann, his son would be Boyce Mann, Jr., and his grandson would be Boyce Mann III.

"You, Jackson," the ambassador turned to him. Jack is all right. Clarence should be, let's see, oh yes, Clear. And you should switch them around, easier for the Koreans. You should tell them you're Jack Clear."

Clarence also smiled and shrugged, and he also thought that would never be; but within weeks he had followed the old man's suggestion and Boyce's example; and for the rest of his life in Korea he was Jack Clear.

Jack would remain in Korea until his death fifteen years later, when his wife Mable and their two daughters left Korea and never returned, having Jack's body embalmed and shipped home to Connecticut. Boyce and Wilma would live there the rest of their lives and be buried there. They would have a son there and name him Boyce, and the son would have two sons there, Boyce and Andrew. Boyce Mann, triplicated, would become a major name in modern Korean history.

The ambassador spent the rest of the evening recounting Korea's story. These people had lived on this peninsula for over five thousand years. The high point of their cultural development was between 668 and 918 AD. They had closed themselves off from foreign trade and cultural exchange in the sixteenth century, much the way Japan did; and the Hermit Kingdom did not open again, and then by outside pressure, until 1866, not quite twenty years ago. It was only in 1880 that the Korean government formed diplomatic relations with the United States, and three years later Dore Mond arrived. The ambassador sat back and smiled at the two men. "Now you are here," he said with a wave of his hand, making it clear that their arrival was due to his influence.

"Here to bring Christ," Clarence said.

"Oh, well, no not exactly," the ambassador said. "I am a Protestant, like you, a Methodist to be exact; but I must be honest and say that the Catholics have been here for over two hundred years. I believe they brought Christ with them." He laughed gently.

"An imperfect Christ," Boyce said.

"Perhaps. But Christ nonetheless." The ambassador shifted in his chair. "The Catholics came through the auspices of a Chinese Christian who had been converted by the Jesuits in Canton. He sneaked in by himself and set up a safe house, then he brought one of the Jesuit priests in under cover. It's a fabulous story. The Chinese Christian was leading the priest, disguised as a Korean farmer, through the streets to the safe house when they were separated by the crush of the crowd. For over an hour the Jesuit was lost, not knowing a word of the language, where he was, how to contact his only friend. Had he been discovered he would have been beheaded on the spot. Then he spotted his friend, they were reunited, and he was hidden away in a secret spot, where he said the first Catholic mass in Korean history later that night. From those two men grew the Catholic Church of Korea, and the Catholics now have a bishop. He conducts mass openly in a church built on the very spot where that first mass was said."

The two Presbyterians were both inspired and threatened by the story. "We were not told there were Catholics here," Clarence said. "We thought we would have an open, clear field."

"Oh, there's no need to be alarmed," the ambassador said. "You're lucky. You will get to know the most open minded Catholic on the face of the earth. Bishop O'Neal is one in a million."

"O'Neal? Boyce said. "Irish?"

"Well, Boston Irish," the ambassador said with a gentle laugh. "Born in Ireland but very much a Boston Yankee. Part of the Irish Potato Diaspora. Excellent man. I'll take you to meet him tomorrow morning." He saw a look of anxiety in the eyes of his two Presbyterians. "You'll get along fine," he assured them. "Remember, you're all working for the good of Jesus Christ and the United States of America."

The next morning at 10:00 the ambassador came for the two men and took them in his carriage, pulled by a matched set of two white horses, though the congested streets to a part of the city that rose slightly above the rest of the plain on which Seoul was built. They stopped in front of a small building built in a vaguely Western style, a building the ambassador called the Cathedral. It was small but was being expanded, and building materials littered the front entrance. The ambassador took them to the left side and up an unimpeded set of stairs, at the top of which a smiling red haired man stood with open arms.

"Your Excellency," the priest said, rushing forward to embrace the ambassador. "How in the world have you been?"

"Fine, your holiness, fine."

"Holiness?" the priest shouted and let out a whoop of laughter. "That's the pope you meant, sir. Me, I'm just poor Father O'Neal. Paddy to you. Nothing holy about me." He patted the ambassador on the back and turned to the two other men. "And these, I gather, are the two Orangemen, eh? Frightened to meet a Papist."

Boyce and Clarence looked from the priest to the ambassador, not knowing what to say, not knowing how to react to this man who said openly what they were both thinking.

"Come now," Paddy O'Neal said, "You know what you are, and I know what I am. And just because I'm Green doesn't mean we can't be friends, brothers even, don't you agree?"

Clarence and Boyce had to smile in spite of themselves, and they responded positively when Paddy hugged them both. He led them and the ambassador through the church to his office, where he served the best coffee they had drunk since they left San Francisco.

When they were seated and sipping the fine brew, Paddy told them about the Catholic work in Korea. "Two hundred years," he said with a sigh. "We've worked here for two centuries. Made two thousand converts. Of course three quarters of them have been martyred. So we have about five hundred now." He let out another whooping laugh.

Clarence and Boyce exchanged glances. So few in so many years, so many massacred. Why the laughter?

"I laugh to keep from crying," Paddy said as if reading their minds. "Of course, with the new government policy, opening up to foreign trade, guaranteeing the safety of missionaries, things should pick up exponentially. You men should be able to make converts much more easily than we did, than we will now, and they will not be killed for their faith."

"You... " Boyce hesitated. "You don't mind our being here?"

"Mind? Why should I mind?" Paddy said. "Oh, I see. Protestant against Catholic, that old rubbish. Listen, I was born in Ireland, and if anyone had a reason to hate Protestants, it would be me. But Good Heavens, men, this is a new land, with millions of lost souls. There's plenty for us all. Let's forget the Green and Orange. Let's save this country for Christ."

"Yes," Clarence said. "Let's do that." He looked at Boyce for assurance, and Boyce shrugged. "I pray so," he said.

Paddy told them he wanted to take them to a special place, and the ambassador excused himself to return to the embassy. Paddy called for a carriage, and the three men rode up to a hill overlooking the River Han. Inside an iron fence were a dozen graves.

"This is the foreigners' cemetery. The Koreans don't want us to bury our dead with theirs. We decided not to make it Catholic or Protestant or Orthodox, just a final resting place for refugees like us. Over here... " He led them across the small square. "... this is the first missionary, Father Gerard, the Jesuit who came from China to conduct the first Catholic mass in Korea. Over here, this is our most recent addition, the Russian ambassador who died earlier this year. His wife didn't want to take him back to Russia. You see the Russian cross."

After they had read the names on all the tombstones, they walked over and looked out across the river.

"So it was you, Father O'Neal, you Catholics who brought Christ to Korea."

"Paddy, please call me Paddy."

"Paddy."

"Actually no," Paddy said with a twinkle in his eye. "Christ was here long before that first Jesuit. We didn't bring him, you didn't bring him, he came long before our time, perhaps during his three days in the grave, when he went to preach to the souls in prison. No, our job is merely to point him out to the people here, to show them that he is already present."

"Yes," Boyce said. "Paddy, I like that idea."

"Me too," Clarence nodded.

"Good. Then let me take you back to the cathedral for lunch. May I offer you with lunch the best rice wine in all of Korea?"

Boyce looked sharply at Clarence. "Uh, Paddy, I think you should know right away, that we do not drink."

"Don't drink?" Paddy croaked. "And you will tell your converts that they cannot drink?"

"That's right," Clarence nodded. "We have to."

"Well then, Brothers, all I can say is that your congregations will be made up entirely of little old ladies—and not many of them."

He let out a wild whooping laugh that echoed from the hill across the river.

3

seoul train

A t the train station Boyce went to the canteen and had tea and a rice roll. Then he went to the counter and bought a ticket to Seoul. His fluent if a bit rusty Korean didn't seem to faze the girl who served him in the café, but it caused the agent some confusion. He asked Boyce how he could help him, speaking English, and he expected Boyce to tell him in English. When Boyce gave his request in Korean, the man frowned and stumbled over his words as he repeated the order. He glanced at Boyce several times as he processed the ticket, and his eyes searched Boyce's face as he handed it to him.

"Thank you," Boyce said as he took it and paid with the cash he had obtained by trading his remaining Yen for Wan before leaving Japan.

"Have you lived in our country long?" the agent asked politely.

"When I was young," Boyce told him.

"Ah, so," the man nodded and smiled. "May I ask your name?"

"Boyce Mann."

"Mann? Oh." The man nodded vigorously. "I have often heard of your family. "Famous American missionaries."

"Are they still known?"

"Oh yes. Studied in schools. Part of our proud heritage."

Boyce smiled and walked out to the departure platform. After a short wait he saw the train for Seoul pull into sight. In a moment he was surrounded by steam and by working men jumping out and making their way hurriedly toward the exit. He waited until the steam and men dissipated, then climbed aboard and found a seat. The train was scheduled to depart at 8:15; and at that precise minute, according to the large clock on the wall outside his car it did exactly that. He had always read that in dictatorships the trains ran on time, and that seemed indeed to be the case.

He had not slept for twenty four hours, and although he felt tired he tried hard not to close his eyes. He wanted to see how the country looked, how it had changed, how it had remained as he remembered it. The trip to Seoul would take four hours, and he would have plenty of time to doze later on. He watched as the train left the city and passed villages and farms, noting the apparent prosperity all around him. The government seemed to be delivering on its promise to promote a higher standard of living. He wondered, however, how the villages and farms beyond the low hills, out of sight of train passengers, might look. He remembered visiting areas off the beaten paths with his father, the poverty, disease, septic conditions that kept Korea a poor country. Maybe the narrow band in sight of train passengers was a façade, a showcase, nothing like the true picture of Yi Dong-ho's "democracy."

He had begun to drift away when a noise, an incident brought him fully awake. Up ahead a stewardess dressed in a uniform was arguing with a passenger, a heavy set man in a blue business suit. She was trying to explain to him that he was in the wrong seat. He resisted her request that he move. He shouted a curse at her and raised a hand to strike her. She stood her ground. The man's companion, also dressed in a business suit, grabbed his arm and forced him to lower it. He held his friend in place and gradually moved him, with physical force and soothing words, away from the seat he had claimed to another one further up the car. The stewardess waited for the cool one to get the hot one settled, then turned briskly and walked down the aisle and out the back door.

Boyce watched as the cool one stood guard in the aisle to make sure his companion did not get up. The cool one glanced back over the car and spotted Boyce, the foreigner. He said something more to his friend and then came slowly down the aisle until he stood in front of Boyce. "Yam solly," he said, bowed, and went back to the seat next to his friend.

Yam solly? Boyce took a moment to figure out what the man had said. Was he Chinese? Was this a Chinese statement? Then it dawned on him that it was English, a Korean's way of saying, "I am sorry." He was apologizing for his friend's behavior. He did not stop to apologize to any of the Korean passengers.

After an hour the train stopped at a moderately large station, and one of the new passengers took the seat opposite Boyce, apparently not concerned that he would be riding backward. He looked Korean but had about his clothing and bearing and the smile he flashed at Boyce a decidedly foreign air. He sat for a long time after the train started moving before he spoke. He continually looked across to Boyce and away again, obviously anxious to speak with him but unsure how to begin. Not himself anxious to pursue a conversation with his mind weary and confused by the sensory data he was trying to process, Boyce waited. At last the man roused his nerve and with a deep breath leaned forward.

"Excuse me, sir, are you American?" He spoke perfect English, with only a slight Korean accent and the usual minute variations of pronunciation.

"I am," Boyce nodded, neither with a smile nor a frown. He was willing to talk but not commit to a long conversation.

"I am English teacher at Koryo University in Seoul," the man said with a proud smile. "I studied at Pennsylvania State University. I received Master's Degree there in English as Second Language."

"You speak quite well," Boyce said in Korean.

"Oh!" The man's eyes widened. "You speak quite well too, my language."

"Thank you."

"But if you please, speak English to me. I like to practice with native speakers, you understand."

"Of course." Boyce smiled at last. He felt like he could spare some time with a man as anxious to please as this one.

"How did you learn such good Korean?"

"I was born here. My parents were missionaries."

"Oh, and what is your name?"

"Boyce Mann."

The man's mouth dropped open, and he stared into Boyce's eyes. He seemed suddenly nervous.

"You come for a visit?" he asked cautiously.

"Yes. I live in North Carolina. I teach art history at Davidson."

"Oh, Duke. Yes, I know about Davidson. You are Wildcat."

"That's right."

"Of course I am Lion, Nittany Lion."

"Of course."

"I have not been back to America, it has been ten years, so tell me, what do Americans hear about Korea?"

"Only about trouble, at times, on the D.M.Z. Oh yes, and about the Reverend Moon Sun-myung."

"Who?"

"The Korean minister. His Unification Church Movement."

"Oh." It was obvious from his expression that the man had not heard about Reverend Moon. His puzzled frown turned quickly to a smile. "When you are in Seoul, perhaps you let me be your guide. City has changed much in last few years. How long have you been away?"

"A quarter of a century."

The man whistled, another sign he was somewhat international. "Oh, well then, you must let me help you."

"Yes, all right. I'd like that. Thank you."

"You have family in Seoul?"

"Only a brother. Andrew Mann. Have you heard of him?"

The man quickly shook his head. "No. Sorry."

"And I have friends there. My mother and father were educators, and many of their students are still around."

"Yes, I'm sure that is true."

"So Seoul has changed. I suppose all of Korea has changed."

"Oh yes. And all for better. We have at last achieved democracy. And as in America, democracy has given us prosperity. We have become what experts call one of the 'little giants,' along with Taiwan and Singapore."

"President Yi, he is a success then?"

"Oh yes. He is the George Washington of Korea."

"Too bad about his wife."

"Oh yes. So so sad. The communists tried to assassinate the president, much as they did President Kennedy, and the shot missed him but hit his wife." The man moved closer to Boyce. "But do you know, he is such a man of discipline and dedication to duty that he went right ahead and delivered his prepared speech after she had been taken to the hospital. He did not know until he finished that she died in ambulance."

"He has carried on, then, as before?"

"Oh yes. His daughter has become First Lady and carries on work of her wonderful mother."

"Miss Yi is a Christian, I believe."

"No, she is a Catholic."

Boyce had forgotten the way Koreans distinguished the two churches. Catholics were Catholics, and Protestants were Christians. He made no effort to correct the man. "Mrs. Yi, her mother, was a Buddhist, I believe."

"Yes. Oh yes, very devout."

"Did that cause any friction in the family?"

"Oh no. Korea has complete freedom of religion. Also the other freedoms found in U.S. Constitution. President Yi presented to us the example of his family to teach us how to get along with each other."

Boyce didn't bring up how the Yi government limited freedom of speech, curtailed freedom of the press, and severely restricted freedom of assembly. But saying that Koreans had freedom of religion evoked his ire.

"Freedom of religion so long as one does not criticize the government," he said with heat.

The man looked shocked and drew back in his seat. "What has religion to do with the government?" he asked. His face revealed surprise and confusion. He was asking the question in all sincerity.

"What do you know about Kim Ji-wan?" Boyce said.

The man's eyes widened, and he raised a forefinger to his lips. "Please," he said, looking all around him, "you must not discuss... that person... in a public place. It is... not wise."

"But you have freedom of speech, don't you?"

"We... it is not wise."

"I have known Kim Ji-wan since I was a child," Boyce said. "She is one of my oldest and dearest friends. I have come here to be of assistance to her in her time of need."

"Oh," the man said. He stood. "I... you must please excuse me, Doctor Boyce. I get off at the next station."

"But you teach in Seoul."

"Yes, but my mother lives here. I must stop and see to her before I return to my post at the university."

"I see. Will you contact me in Seoul, to be my guide? I will be staying at the Chosun Hotel."

"Yes. I promise to do that. Thank you, sir, I will see you again soon, sir."

He pushed quickly out into the aisle and gave Boyce a bow and a wave of his hand before turning and hurrying out of the car.

It was several minutes before the train began to slow for the next station, but Boyce took the man at his word that he was stopping to visit his mother. At the station several people left the car and several came in. Boyce looked idly out the streaky window to see if he could spot the man but saw nothing of him. There was a throng of people on the platform. By mid morning people were ready to travel. He needed to relieve himself but knew it was against the law to use train toilets in stations, so he waited.

When the train had moved out of the station and was fully out into the countryside, he got up and went to the facilities between cars. As he started to open the toilet door he glanced into the next car, which had tables for dining, and saw the man drinking a cup of tea.

Boyce stood looking at him through the glass until the man glanced up and saw him. Boyce winked and waved to him. The man looked shocked, then chagrined, and then he dropped his eyes. Boyce chuckled to himself and went into the toilet. When he came out a few minutes later the man was gone.

4

manns

The two missionary wives arrived early in 1888. By that time Boyce and Jack had found housing, started conducting regular church services, and had won a dozen converts. Wilma McMann and Mable Jackson, who had lived for three years at a Japanese mission, found living conditions in Korea primitive; but neither complained. Certain that this was God's will for them, they set to work being good helpmates to husbands with a divine mission.

The Presbyterian property was only four square acres, and the church and two residences were joined by an open air breezeway. Each woman had her own kitchen and living space, but they alternated preparing meals for both couples to share. As the number of converts increased, they found among them Korean women to help them shop and keep the premises clean.

Within a year Jack and Mable had a daughter, with Wilma serving as mid wife at the birth, a skill she had learned during the time she and Boyce prepared for their work in Korea. Two years later came another Jackson daughter. Although they wanted children, Boyce and Wilma went year after year without conception. Nothing in Korean society was secret or out of bounds for discussion, and so the Korean women who came to church and helped with shopping and cleaning frankly expressed their disappointment and their pity for Wilma. A woman should have children, they told her, for without them she was a burden to her husband. The Korean men who attended church with their wives and helped maintain and guard the buildings were just as frank with Boyce. To be fully a man he must father children, and far better if the children were males. What a shame he was childless. What a shame he did not have a son.

During the year 1894 Jack's family took their first furlough and spent the year touring the United States, speaking to Presbyterian churches and conferences, describing their work in Korea, asking for support. As soon as they returned it was Boyce's turn; and during the year 1895 he and Wilma returned to America for the same round of tours and talks. While at home in New Jersey Wilma asked advice and was told to see a doctor who specialized in what were called "women's problems."

"Mrs. McMann," he told her after he had given her a complete physical examination, one that embarrassed her because she had never had such an examination before, "there is no reason for you not to conceive and produce a healthy child. You are normal in every way. You are healthy. You are fertile."

"Then what's wrong?" she asked him, close to tears. "I have tried all the remedies for barrenness my own mother and the women in Korea to whom I am a minister have to offer. None of them has had any effect."

"No, not likely," the doctor smiled. He guessed that the remedies she had been offered were medieval. American folk remedies certainly were, and he could imagine that Korean one would be even more.

"Then what am I to do?" she asked.

"I suspect the problem is that you work too hard, that you do not get enough rest, and that you are anxious each time you have sexual intercourse to get back to the work of the mission. I suspect also that you want a child so badly that you are trying to conceive a bit too desperately. Am I partially correct?

She dropped her eyes.

"So what I suggest you do is take more time, linger over sex, enjoy it more, stay put, let yourself fall asleep, after you have received your husband's seed."

She was embarrassed by the doctor's words. No one had ever spoken to her that way, not her mother, not her husband, not any of the Korean women who gave her advice. She had been told that he was a modern physician who spoke bluntly, but she was not quite prepared for words like these.

"Have sex as often as you can, more than once at a time, then lie there for as long as you can, go to sleep if possible, lie there until you cannot wait to urinate any longer. All right?"

These words embarrassed her even more. She nodded without speaking, stood, thanked the doctor, avoiding his eyes, and left as quickly as possible.

While they were away, letters from the Jacksons told them about the Japanese encroachments on the peninsula; and they began making plans to return earlier than they had planned, so as to be with their converts in case there was violence. They were afraid the shipping lanes would be affected by the conflict; but they were not. They changed boats in Japan as easily on the return trip as on the way out. The Japanese officials seemed anxious not to offend their American trading partners. Events in Asia should be kept purely Asian.

On the return voyage, despite fears of trouble to come, Wilma encouraged Boyce to rest up for the ordeal ahead, not to think about what might happen but just assure that he was physically prepared for it. She urged him to skip breakfast each morning, to make excuses to the captain, and to sleep late. She also made sure that each of the long mornings abed she aroused him and guided him into her more than once each time and that each time he fully completed his mission. Six weeks after they arrived back in Seoul she was able to announce to Boyce and then to the Korean women, who announced it to the Korean men, that she was pregnant. The entire church rejoiced. Late in August 1896 she gave birth to a boy, and he was given his father's adopted name, Boyce Mann, Jr. Try as she might to conceive again in years to come, he was to be her only child. She explained it to herself by saying that she and her husband never again spent two weeks together on the ocean.

Boyce Jr. was nine years old when his father baptized him along with seven other recent converts in the Han River in 1905, the year the Japanese won their war with Russia, the first Asian nation to defeat an European one, giving them what they considered a green light to be the imperial power in the East. He was fourteen in 1910 when Japan officially annexed Korea into the Japanese Empire, after which Koreans were required to learn and speak Japanese and were fined if caught speaking Korean. Koreans were to become Japanese, culturally and linguistically. Still anxious to keep good relations with the United States, Japanese officials who ran Seoul and the rest of the peninsula treated the missionaries with deference so long as they did not oppose the regime. They were told that they might conduct church services in English or Japanese but not in Korean, which meant that many of their members had trouble understanding the hymns or sermons. The Manns and the Jacksons learned Japanese in order to negotiate with the overlords, but services were all conducted in English. Korean was not brought back until 1945.

Boyce Mann, Jr. left Korea for the first time in 1914, aged 18, on his way to study at Princeton. He arrived there in late June, at the outbreak of war in Europe; but despite the several times when it appeared the U.S. might get involved, he paid little attention. He was too busy with his studies and his social life. As he grew up in Korea his parents had made it clear to him that he was not to touch Korean girls, that this was taboo, something that would compromise their mission; and so during his first three years of college he made up for lost time. He went to as many parties as possible, romanced as many girls as he could meet, all of them white, and at age 21 was deeply, madly in love with a southern belle who was studying at Mount Holyoke. Her name was Emily Anderson, she came in time to share his dream of going to Korea to work with the mission, and he wrote to his parents that he hoped to marry her as soon as he graduated in the spring of 1918.

World affairs intervened. Two months before he finished his junior year at Princeton, already making plans for marriage, then seminary, then return to what he considered his homeland, President Wilson asked for a declaration of war against Germany. The United States was in the Great War. When he heard the news and saw the excitement all around him, Boyce felt stirrings he had never before known. Although he knew he was an American, simply born in Korea, he had never felt truly American, certainly not enough to defend this country in time of war; but now he had emotions he could not explain. He tried the next time he visited Emily at Mount Holyoke.

"I... feel torn," he said. "I have always believed I was a pacifist, and I have not considered myself fully a Yankee. But it's as though one of my family has been attacked. I am angry at the Germans. I want to defend our honor. What am I to do?"

Emily nodded and smiled. She was the granddaughter of an officer in the Confederate army; and like many southern families hers had transferred allegiance from the lost cause of southern independence to a vivid patriotism for the nation they were forced to rejoin in 1865.

"What is your heart telling you to do, Boyce?" she said.

"It's... I don't know... I think it's telling me to volunteer, to go and fight; but my mind is telling me that war is futile and that I should protest the violence by speaking out against it."

"I say follow your heart. My heart tells me to marry you and go to Korea, and that trumps my mind which tells me to marry a nice boy from Virginia who will keep me in the comfort to which I have become accustomed. I am listening to my heart, you must listen to yours."

In the end the selective service in Princeton made the choice for him. He was summoned for a physical examination, passed it easily, and was ordered to report for training at a New Jersey base. Since his heart was telling him the same thing, he made no protest. He talked with the dean and learned that Princeton was giving a year's credit to any student who saw active service and that at commencement 1918, whether he were on campus or not, he would be granted his degree.

He then went directly to Mount Holyoke and asked Emily to marry him. She seemed puzzled. "Of course I will, Boyce," she said. "I told you that when you first asked me."

"No," he said. "Not when we planned. Now. I might not come home, at least not in one piece. I want you so much, I want us to join our hearts and bodies completely, to have a few days, if that's all we can manage, together, just the two of us. Let's do it now, before it's forever too late."

"Yes," Emily said. "Yes, we must."

Without telling either family, they made the arrangements and were married by a New Jersey justice of the peace in early June. By the first of July Boyce was in uniform, and Emily was home in Virginia, with the promise that whatever happened she would be his only love and that forever.

The two years he spent crossing the Atlantic to England, then fighting in France, then mopping up in Germany changed him forever. The shock of battle, the carnage, the smell of rotting bodies, the smoke from burned out cities, the consummate waste of human life and heritage brought him to a point where he cared not whether he lived or died. He took his first drink of alcohol and for a time drowned his anguish in it. He took comfort in the arms of a French woman who traded her body for his food rations. He compared the French and Germans and concluded that his country had sent him into battle for the wrong nation against the wrong nation. He admired the Germans he had helped kill more than the French he had helped defend. On a devastated hillside he raised his fist to the heavens and cried out, "My God, My God, why hast thou forsaken me?" He felt he had lost his faith.

His troop ship docked in New York in early summer 1920, and as soon as he reported to the old base in New Jersey he was handed a letter from his mother. He had heard nothing from Korea for almost two years; and the news he now read was all bad. There had been an uprising in Seoul. Koreans, inspired by the talk of national self determination at Versailles, had declared their independence from Japan. The Japanese authorities had cracked down with a severity never known there. Hundreds were arrested, many of them summarily executed. The Japanese blamed "foreign" influences for the rebellion. They noted that many of the Korean rebels were Christians, and they surmised from that fact that missionaries had inspired the rising. After all, it was President Woodrow Wilson, a Presbyterian, who called for self determination of oppressed people, although he refused to admit that American Negroes were oppressed.

A newspaper clipping, from an English press in Japan, followed the first page of the letter. Boyce Mann, born in New Jersey in 1862, Christian missionary to Korea since 1885, was one of the foreigners arrested. He was being held for trial. If found guilty, he would not be executed, since he was an American citizen; but he and his wife would be immediately expelled. They would be put aboard a ship headed for the United States and forever banned from reentry to Korea.

The second page was a passionate plea for Boyce to come home, to save his father, to do what he could to prevent this tragedy. She did not know where he was, whether he was alive or dead; but she trusted that if he were alive and received this message God would somehow give him passage to come home. She placed her faith in God the Father and his Son the Lord Jesus Christ.

Boyce went immediately to the nearest federal building and asked how long it would take to process papers for him to return to Korea. After hearing why he wanted to go, the official told him that it would be impossible. U.S. relations with Japan were at a critical juncture; and the Japanese were convinced that Reverend Mann was at least partly responsible for the uprising against the empire. They would not let his son return to Korea at the present time, probably not for many months or even years. Boyce asked if the government had late news about his father, and the man said no, but Boyce could tell by the look in his eye that he was holding back information.

That night Boyce, his heart overflowing with anguish, took a walk through the town that abutted the army base. He had no idea how his parents were faring, since the letter was six weeks old. He had no idea where Emily was and whether she would still love the fallen angel she had married two years before, now a rotten sinner who had lost his faith. He didn't know how to get home or what he would or could do if and when he got there. He pushed his way into a tavern crowded with soldiers, elbowed his way to the bar, and ordered a drink.

He thought how disappointed his father and mother would be if they knew he went to bars, let alone drank spirits. He swallowed his whiskey, ordered a second, finished it, and leaned back against the bar in a rising mental fog to look around the room. Clumps of men and women were chatting in various spots, and he wandered over to the one that seemed the most lively. He wanted to be among people, listen to them talking, forget his worries.

A bespeckled young soldier was in the middle of a lecture, to which some of his listeners were agreeing and some disagreeing, on "that silly assed fool Woodrow Wilson." Boyce started to move on, but the boy was provocative. "All I'm saying," the boy preached, "is that it's dumb as hell to go half way around the globe to save people who are too stupid to save themselves. All this crusading, making the world safe for democracy, waging a war to end all wars, it's idiotic. Why, we're led to the slaughter by a damned missionary. Wilson is a Methodist or some other crazy damned thing, and he's delusional, he thinks he's the twentieth century's Prince of Peace. To hell with him!" There followed his pronouncement both applause and jeers.

Boyce felt a stirring in his chest. Once again his head and his heart were in conflict. His brain knew the boy was right, that all efforts to save the world were in vain, that crusaders were all either naïve or insane, that the war he had fought and the mission his parents had taken were foolish wastes of talent and energy. Yet his heart wanted desperately to say it was not true. He was torn, just as he had been when America entered the war. Then he had followed his heart, and that had led to disaster, to a loss of faith in things of the heart. Now he was unsure whether to follow his heart a second time or be reasonable.

He was also embarrassed by his tendency to swing so wildly from one emotion to another. In March 1917 he was apathetic about the war, apathetic about America and its role in the world order; and in April 1917 he was prepared to risk his life for the country he had not known until he was eighteen. In March 1918 he believed in God and the basic goodness of man and the righteous cause of people like his parents; in November 1918 he had lost faith in all three and descended into the depths of moral hell. Now, after listening to this brief tirade he felt righteous indignation and a need to speak up for God, his parents, and the mission they had taken. Not finding the words, more than a bit tipsy from the whiskey, he resorted to raw emotion. He rushed toward the speaker and knocked him to the floor. There followed a general melee, with bloodshed, broken up finally by military police.

The next morning Boyce was released from the brig, and the provost officer assured him that this one silly act would not tarnish his distinguished war record, that the army expected outbursts of this sort from men trained to fight, that it would be abnormal if occasionally they didn't resort to fisticuffs. Still sore from his bruises and still slightly hung over, he wrote Emily a long letter. He told her he was home and would be released from the army in another week. He also told her about his father's arrest and that he was more committed than ever to returning to Korea as a missionary and that he planned to enter Princeton Divinity School in September. He told her how much he loved her and wanted her to come to him as soon as she could. After posting that letter he wrote a second one to his mother, telling her also that he was in New Jersey and asking for news about his father, assuring her that if it were possible he would come home immediately. Then he waited and stewed.

Reunited with Emily, who refused to let him confess his wartime sins, who accepted him just as he was, with a steady stream of letters keeping him informed about his father's ordeal, he began his theological studies. He rejoiced when the next year his father was released from prison, but he grieved when his mother described how broken he was. Only 58, he looked twenty years older that that. He could not preach or teach, and he spent much of each day in bed. But she encouraged Boyce to finish his studies and apply to the Presbyterian Mission Board to appoint him to Korea and come home when he was ready to assume his father's job in the church. Boyce did as he was told, finished his degree, got his appointment, and arrived in Seoul with Emily in time to spend nine months with his father before the older man died in 1924 at the age of 62.

The first Boyce Mann was buried in the foreigner's cemetery, where Paddy O'Neal had taken him on his second day in Korea. It was by then called Missionary Ridge. Paddy attended, elderly now, wearing secular clothing to avoid being too conspicuous; and after the interment he came up to give the second Boyce

Mann a hug. Boyce had known Father Paddy since he was a boy, and feeling his embrace brought tears to his eyes.

"Pardon the pun, but he was a real man, that Boyce Mann," Paddy said with a twinkle in his eye. "You know how much I loved him."

"Yes, I know," Boyce said.

"Korea killed him. But he wouldn't have wanted it any other way."

"Yes."

"Someday the whole nation will know what he did and praise his name for it, you do know that."

"I do. I believe it."

"Good." Paddy patted his back. "Good." He looked him in the face. "Now you carry on for him, Boyce my boy, you carry on for him."

"I will."

For the next decade everything Boyce did was for his father. He started a seminary to train Korean ministers, as his father had dreamed of doing. He was its first teacher and as he added faculty he served as its first dean. He gradually constructed a liberal arts curriculum, and he then gave over his deanship to a Korean man and became head of the first college for men in Korea. Following its success, he founded an adjoining college for women, naming a female Korean convert who had studied at Davidson College under his father's sponsorship as its head. The Mann name became an integral part of Korean history.

With his mother's health declining, he encouraged Emily to take more responsibility with the orphanage, and when his mother died in 1927, when she was only 62, Emily became its head. He and Emily presided over his mother's burial on the hill beside his father. Now there was a second Reverend and Mrs.

Boyce Mann in charge of the Presbyterian mission to the Land of the Morning Calm.

Without sacrificing his dignity or compromising his theology, he carefully kept channels of communication open with the Japanese government. He made it clear that his church and schools would preach the Gospel in all its variety of interpretations and not flinch from taking moral stands but that he would not purposely provoke an uprising against the regime. In return the Japanese governor-general gave his minions instructions to leave the church alone.

In 1928 Bishop Patrick O'Neal died. Boyce and Emily not only attended his funeral at the Catholic Cathedral but marched in the procession from the church to Missionary Ridge, to what had come to be called the Catholic Section of it, for the burial. Both Catholics and Protestants looked askance at this gesture; but Boyce announced from the pulpit the next Sunday that the bishop was his father's friend and supporter and that he had attended him in death out of respect for his contribution to the evangelization of Korea.

Sadly the procession from church to graveyard was conducted in constant rainfall, and both Boyce and Emily came down severe colds which in time turned into pneumonia. Emily was pregnant, having waited nine years to conceive a child, longer than his parents had waited for a baby, and during her illness she miscarried. For nearly a year she grieved and could hardly carry on her work with the orphanage; but at Christmas 1929 she told Boyce with a happy whoop that she was once more pregnant. Boyce Mann III was born in 1930, with Andrew coming four years later. The name would go forward.

In 1937 Japan went to war with China, and for the first time Korean men were forcibly inducted into the Japanese Imperial

Army. Some of Boyce's most capable church members found themselves in uniform and headed for the Chinese War zone. Boyce paid an official visit to the Japanese Governor-General to protest the policy.

"These men are being drafted against their wills. They are Koreans and do not wish to be Japanese soldiers," he said as forcefully as possible without raising his voice.

"They are Japanese citizens," the Governor-General said, softly sipping a cup of imported tea.

"Many of them are pacifists. I myself am a pacifist. I served the United States in the Great War, and it made me sick of conflict. I have taught my people to feel the same way. Do you not have an exception for pacifists?"

"We recognize no such philosophy. We call pacifism cowardice."

"But you do permit freedom of religious choice and worship. What if a man's faith tells him serving as a soldier, where he might be required to kill other human beings, is evil?"

"Is your church officially pacifist, Reverend Doctor Mann?" the Governor-General asked with a raised eyebrow. "I have never heard so. I know about Quakers, but you are not Quakers. Your people have always fought in wars, as you did twenty years past."

"We are not official pacifists, no, but we do believe that killing is wrong. 'Thou shalt not kill,' says our Bible."

"Do you eat meat?"

"We do."

"Then you kill."

"Not human beings."

"Oh, sir," the Governor-General smiled, "The Chinese are not human."

Boyce and his church remained under close scrutiny for the next four years, as the war in China grew hotter and word reached him through American sources of Japanese atrocities in Chinese cities. The scrutiny only increased after December 7, 1941, when the United States and Japan went to war. More and more of Boyce's church members were drafted. Most Koreans, especially the Christians, both Protestant and Catholic, tried their best to protect him and Emily and the boys, but they were warned not to venture off church property for fear of being attacked by Koreans hoping to ingratiate themselves to the Japanese. They remained in the orphanage most days and only went to the church or the schools by night. Enrollment in both the boys and girls schools declined precipitously due to impressments and lack of money to pay tuition.

Only the orphanage grew, with more and more Korean children being abandoned and left destitute. It was during the war years that Emily came to depend ever more on the little girl who became her surrogate daughter, Kim Ji-wan. Kim had been brought to Emily in 1932, when she was still a baby, and she had quickly become Emily's favorite among the orphans. Emily gave her the family name Kim because one fifth of the Korean population had that name and it was a safe guess that this was her parents' name. "Ji-wan" had the connotation of "loved one," and that is what the little girl was to Emily. After Andrew was born Emily knew that at age 38 she would have no more children, never have the daughter she so much wanted, and Ji-wan fill the empty space in her heart.

Ji-wan was just a bit younger than Emily's older son Boyce, and the two of them grew up together. Ji-wan was Boyce's first romantic interest. When Boyce was twelve, as the war between

America and Japan began to reverberate throughout Korea, Boyce told his father that he was in love.

"You are?" his father said, first smiling, then frowning. "But with whom? There are no American girls here."

"I'm in love with Ji-wan, father," Boyce laughed.

"Ji-wan? No, no you can't be, son. She is... not one of us."

"What do you mean? She speaks English. She is a Christian."

"Yes, but she is Korean. We have a rule, son, that no missionary ever, ever looks with desire at a native person."

"I... I don't understand."

"You will, son. In time you will."

Boyce was careful not to speak with his father again about Ji-wan; but he continued to love her, and the two of them spent ever more time together. It was in the spring of 1945, while they hid behind the altar in the church, terrified by bombs raining down on Seoul, American bombs aimed at the Japanese army, that they made love for the first and last time. Neither ever mentioned it, and after Boyce left for Princeton three years later, they never saw each other again. Yet in all the conversations they had before he left and in all the letters they exchanged while he was away were unspoken and unwritten intimacies that never died. Boyce still loved Ji-wan as he had never loved another woman.

One of Boyce's most vivid memories was the day the American army marched into Seoul. He was surprised to see how unkempt they looked. The Japanese army had marched out the day before all spit and polish, clean shaven, with their uniforms shaped to their bodies and spotless. The Americans were unshaven, not particularly clean, and their shirt tails hung down over their hips. Many of them were chewing gum. Boyce remembered little

Korean boys asking how on earth this bunch of hoodlums had defeated the Japanese.

However they had managed to do it, America had won, the Japanese had lost, and the long nightmare was over. His father called him and Andrew to his side and spoke to them with eyes shining with pleasure.

"Boys, this is the dawning of a new age. It may not be the arrival of the Kingdom of God, but it will make that arrival possible. We will live to see it."

Always the teacher, his father never missed an opportunity to teach his sons new words. "Boys, do you know the word 'cynosure'?" he asked them.

"It means you have an office but don't have to do any work," Boyce said.

"No," his father laughed. "That's a sinecure: s-i-n-e-c-u-r-e. This word I mean is c-y-n-o-s-u-r-e. Any ideas?"

They both shook their heads.

"The root is the Latin for dog. A cynosure is a lead dog, in a dog sled team. Well that is what we are. We are the cynosures, the lead dogs in a new age. God put us here at this particular time to bring in a new Korea. It will be a Korea that is independent, united, democratic, and Christian. You boys will go home, get your education, and return to lead this country into the modern age. You promise to do that?"

The two boys nodded and smiled. Their father, their country, their God all depended on them.

5

seoul sunday

oyce's train arrived at Seoul Station a tad before 2:00; and as tired as he was he wasted no time finding a taxi stand and getting to the Chosun Hotel. Although he desperately needed to sleep, he remained alert through the ride across town, comparing the Seoul he saw passing his window to the one he had known a quarter century before. The Japanese built structures had stood the test of time and the elements better than the newer ones. Streets and sidewalks were both much more crowded, more cars, more people. Yet the signs, the faces, the odors were much the same. Knowing that the American military base in the heart of Seoul had grown into a city unto itself, he was surprised to see almost no foreign faces in the crowds. Korean was still, as it had been when he left, largely Korean. Pedestrians stared at his unusual face as his cab passed them.

Both the cab driver and then the hotel desk clerk were surprised that he spoke Korean. He figured he might as well get used to this shock, since it was bound to recur every time he opened his mouth as long as he stayed in the country. He answered each one's questions with as few words as possible.As soon as he was shown his room he fell across the bed, without undressing, and went quickly into a deep sleep.

He woke at 9:00, so said his wrist watch, and he was starving. He washed his face and gave his suit a quick realignment and made his way down to the lobby. He thought it best to eat in rather than go looking for food on the street.

"Your dining room... is where?" he asked the desk clerk, a new one, who predictably looked up in surprise at his Korean.

"Uh, well, sir... " The man looked embarrassed. "You see, we just closed the dining room."

"Oh," Boyce nodded. "Well, thank you anyway." He started toward the front door.

The clerk rushed around from behind his desk, caught up with Boyce, and took his arm. "But sir, please wait. It's best for you not to go outside, not this time of night. Not on a Saturday. The drinking and all."

He led Boyce by the arm back to the dining room. The door was closed, but the clerk knocked until a waiter came and opened it. He explained that this was an honored guest—a member of the Mann family—and that he needed a good meal. Boyce wondered at the speed with which his identify had spread. The waiter, angry at the intrusion at first, nodded vigorously when he heard who Boyce was and led him to a table. Boyce heard him in the kitchen ordering the cook to unpack the food and prepare a meal. In short order the waiter brought him a plate with barley water to drink—apparently he knew the Manns did not drink wine—and proudly stood behind him as he ate. When he had finished he told the waiter to put the meal on his hotel bill and handed him a generous tip. The waiter assured him he would see about the bill and with great aplomb refused to accept the tip.

Boyce was unaccustomed to Korean food. In the States, to avoid being labeled Korean, with all the stereotypes that entailed, he had assiduously avoided going to Korean restaurants or preparing it for himself. Now the excessive spices bore heavily on his stomach. Without returning to the desk, he went out a side door to the street. He found it as crowded at 10:00 as it had been at 2:00. He was so accustomed to living in American cities, where everyone went to roost at sundown and the streets were deserted, that finding such hordes of people at night was a mild surprise. He also noticed, as the clerk had warned, that there was an alarming degree of public intoxication.

He had read in one of his grandfather's earliest reports to the Presbyterian Missions Board the observation and speculation of an American and a tee-totaler that the Koreans had a natural tendency to drunkenness. His grandfather believed that this was due to the genetic kinship Koreans had to American Indians, who were also unable to control their appetite for demon rum. He said he hoped American trade merchants would control the flow of foreign alcohol into the peninsula and predicted that should the supply increase and Koreans become more affluent, it would cause an alcoholic epidemic. Boyce observed that apparently his grandfather's prophecy, if not necessarily his theory about genetics, had proven accurate.

Despite the hustle and chaos on the streets, Boyce was finally able to get his bearings, using the landmark monuments he remembered from his youth as his guides. He passed the Great South Gate to the city, the Great East Gate, where Koreans had once brought tribute money to Chinese soldiers to prevent them from looting the city, and at last found himself at the gates to the palace where in 1919 Koreans had declared independence from Japan. At this very spot his grandfather had stood with his Korean converts, and here he had been arrested, for all intents and purposes ending his life. Boyce was standing lost in thought, recalling the family stories about the event, when a police officer came up to him and spoke in English: "Sir, you must leave now."

"Is that so?" Boyce said in Korean. Again the startled expression. "What have I done wrong?"

"Nothing, sir," he cop said, still speaking English. "It's just that we have a curfew beginning in a half hour, and no one is allowed on the streets from then until 7:00 a.m. in the morning."

"Oh, I see," Boyce said in Korean. "I am quite a distance from my hotel."

"Which hotel?" the cop said in English. He could not accept the fact that a man with Boyce's face could speak Korean, even though he heard him do it.

"The Chosun."

"Good." The cop walked out into the street, raised his arm to a passing car, blew his whistle, and ordered the driver to pull over. "Take his gentleman to the Chosun Hotel," he ordered the driver.

The driver shook his head vigorously. "That is far out of my way," he said. "I have a short enough time to get home as it is, and going there will make me risk being caught out after curfew."

"Take him to the Chosun Hotel!" the cop ordered and frowned down at the man. "Do as I say."

The man started to argue, but the cop gave him a warning look. "Open the door and get in," he said to Boyce.

"But I don't want the man to be late," Boyce said.

"He won't be late. Get in."

Boyce opened the door and got in beside the man. The cop signaled for them to be off, and the driver spun his wheels in anger as he followed orders. After a block Boyce tried to apologize, but the man shook his head vigorously. He drove like one demon possessed through the streets crowded with people scurrying to get inside by the top of the hour, screeched to a halt at the hotel, and as soon as Boyce stepped out he spun his wheels leaving. Boyce walked on shaking legs into the hotel lobby.

The clerk came out to meet him. "I hope you were not in any way injured during your walk," he said.

"No," Boyce said. "I was warmly welcomed home."

At eight the next morning, having eaten a hotel breakfast of rice and eggs, Boyce took a cab to the Seoul Presbyterian Church, which was an outgrowth of the small one his grandfather had founded ninety years before. It was a huge edifice, seating as many as four thousand people, offering four services each Sunday morning to accommodate the nearly twelve thousand who attended regularly. He had chosen the first of the four services because he assumed it would be the least crowded. He was wrong. The sanctuary was full.

A Korean usher spotted him and rush up to welcome him with a handshake. In English he offered to take Boyce to the visitors' section, where there were headsets to listen to a simultaneous translation. Boyce politely declined, speaking Korean, and said that he preferred to listen without aid. The usher backed away from him, squinted, and said, "Are you... are you young Boyce Mann?"

Boyce smiled. "Not so young, but I am Boyce Mann."

The usher bowed and led him to a row near the front of the church. He shooed the family sitting on the aisle over and sat Boyce down. "Please enjoy the worship service," he said.

Boyce turned to apologize to the ousted family, but they merely smiled and nodded a welcome. He tried to concentrate, to prepare himself for the service, but out of the corner of his eyes he watched the usher make his way around the church, telling all the other ushers about him, and watching the word spread through the congregation. As soon as the team of five ministers entered and took their seats on the podium, one of the ushers went up and whispered the same message to them. They all looked at Boyce and smiled. Boyce recognized only one of the ministers, the eldest, who was much changed but still bore a resemblance of the young man in his thirties Boyce had known as a boy. He had kept up with the career of Pastor Ju Si-wan and knew that he was now senior minister of Seoul Presbyterian Church.

Boyce noted at the front of the sanctuary, above the choir, above the cross, a large picture of Jesus. He was a Renaissance Italian, painted by a mediocre nineteenth century artist imitating a sculpture by Michelangelo. It was the same likeness his grandfather had brought with him, in a much small version, when he arrived from America. It had hung in the first small church, and now in a blow up it hung in the enormous church that succeeded it. Most Koreans had no idea how Jesus actually looked—nor did most Americans—but this was their image.

The hymns were in Korean, all but one, the traditional Scottish air *Amazing Grace*, which was sung in English. He wondered how many of the worshippers knew what the words meant. When Pastor Ju introduced his Biblical text, "Render unto God that which is God's and unto Caesar that which is Caesar's," he read it first in English and then translated it into Korean. In America the pastors sometimes read texts in Greek and translated them into English so that parishioners could understand. In Korea English was Greek, the original language of their Bible.

Pastor Ju's sermon was brief, only a preface really to a longer one given after the collection plates went around by one of his younger assistants. He looked small and drawn, a mere wispy memory of the vigorous man Boyce remembered. He had been one of his father's converts, born around the turn of the century, converted when he was 25, one of the first native born Koreans to be ordained a minister in the church. He had volunteered to go north and start a mission in Pyong-yang and was there when the Korean War began in 1950. He and his congregation had fled south during the war and joined forces with the Seoul Church to fight the communists. Because his own converts outnumbered the decimated Seoul congregation, Ju was chosen to replace Boyce's father when he died. He was now in his mid seventies and frail, but he continued to be senior minister, and while his sermons were brief, they were the centerpieces of the four Sunday services.

His sermon employed veiled language to speak of the crisis the church faced with the imprisonment of Kim Ji-wan. He did not mention her name, but he spoke of "one of our flock who is suffering." He said he understood how the members felt, why they did not agree on what should be done. He recounted the story of Paul and Silas in the Philippian jail and pointed out that they had not tried to escape but instead had waited for God to bring an earthquake to open their cell door, that they had used the opportunity to bring salvation to the jailer and his family. He repeated his text and emphasized that Christians must render to God that which was God's but also render to Caesar that which was Caesar's. He sighed and returned to his seat without hammering in the nail.

When the final prayer ended, Boyce stepped out into the aisle and met face to face with the usher. "Doctor Mann," the usher said, "Pastor Ju would like to talk with you."

"Of course," Boyce said. "Where?"

"Follow me."

The usher led Boyce through the crowd of smiling Christians, around the front of the podium, and through a door to the area behind the choir. Down a darkened hallway they walked, and with a soft tap he opened a door and led Boyce into a simple but cozy study. Pastor Ju stood and came to meet Boyce. He opened his arms and embraced him, calling him "my son, my son," and had him take a seat beside his own. Boyce noted that on the wall behind Ju's chair was a small version of the Italian Jesus. It looked old enough to be the one his grandfather brought from America in 1885.

"Would you like tea?" Ju said.

"Pastor Ju, I have lived in America a long time, where the tea is not as good as it is here. I would love some of the real thing."

Pastor Ju laughed and clapped his hands. A serving lady entered, and he instructed her to bring the very best tea for him and his honored guest.

"It is so good, so very good to see you again," Ju said. He spoke Korean, knowing that Boyce would understand him.

"I am glad to see you again too," Boyce said.

"You bring back the past," Ju said. "I have such fond memories of your parents, and even of your grandparents." He smiled. "Yes, I remember all of them well." He leaned forward. "Your grandfather became good friends to the king, did you know this, and once when there were threats of an uprising against him, your grandfather slept by the king's bed, with his American six shooter under his pillow, to kill any intruder."

"My goodness. I never knew that."

"Your grandmother, who knew midwifery, helped in the birth of two of the royal children, two who lived by the way because of her use of sterile instruments. Two others had died of infections."

"That I had heard."

"Your father, what a great man he was, he recommended me for ordination, the first Korean to be a Presbyterian minister. He wrote home and raised the money to help me go north and start my mission. When I returned south during the war he was ill and he recommended that the church make me the pastor to succeed him."

You have done a marvelous job, Pastor Ju."

Ju laughed. "No, my son, God has done a marvelous job."

"Yes."

"My task now is to prepare the church for the time I will go up there."

"Back to the north?"

"Oh no, although I wish I could. No, when I go up to heaven."

"May that be many years from now," Boyce said.

The tea came, and Ju poured them each a cup. After he sat back, he said, "What do Americans think of Reverend Moon?"

"They find him amusing. They think he represents Korean religion."

"The merging of all religious beliefs, without regard to the truth or falsehood of any? Choosing mates for his followers? The claim that he is God's only true voice on earth?"

"Yes."

"Too bad really. I knew him, you know, and believe me he is not a moral man. He is evil."

"That was my guess."

Ju was silent for a moment, then he continued: "Are you here, have you returned, because of Kim Ji-wan?"

"Yes."

Ju was silent for a longer time, sipping his tea. Finally he spoke, not to give advice but to issue a gentle warning. "Be careful, my son, be careful."

"Yes, I will," Boyce assured him.

"Our church has made a bargain with the Yi government. Some call it demonic, I call it practical. It is not as bad as the one your father had to make with the Japanese. Don't take any chances here, son, we do not need any more martyrs, we have had enough, including your dear mother. We certainly do not need any white messiahs." Behind him the Italian Jesus smiled.

Ju finished his tea. "In a moment I must go. The next service is about to begin, and although I contribute very little, each congregation expects to see me. If I am not there, they worry."

"So would I."

Ju laughed. "Have you seen Andrew?"

"No. He doesn't know I'm here."

"Oh, I'm sure he knows. The authorities keep close tabs. But he has not contacted you?"

"No."

"Nor you him?"

"No."

Ju stood up. "Well, I must remedy that." He walked to his desk and took up his telephone, then dialed a number. He waited. "Andrew? It is Ju Si-wan. Yes, yes, well. We have missed you." He switched to English: "Long time, no see, eh?" Back to Korean.

"Your brother is here. So you knew. He wants to see you. Would you like to talk with him?" He frowned. "Well, where would you like to meet?" A long pause, waiting for a response. "Yes. All right. Good. I'll tell him. I hope to see you again in church soon."

Ju hung up and came back to Boyce. "He will come to your hotel at noon, and you will have lunch."

"Does he know the hotel?"

"He said the Chosun."

"That's right."

As they left the office, Ju to the sanctuary and Boyce to the outer door, the pastor touched him lightly on the arm. "Do not be too surprised when you see your brother. Remember he has had a hard life."

At noon the telephone in Boyce's room rang. A desk clerk told him that his brother was waiting for him in the lobby.

"Tell him to come up," Boyce said.

After a moment the clerk said, "He prefers that you come down, sir."

Boyce took the stairs instead of the elevator, and when he came into the lobby he saw Andrew waiting for him near the elevator, watching the door. He was able to look him over for a moment without letting him know he was being watched. Andrew wore a suit, but it was even more frayed and shapeless than Boyce's, as if the brothers competed to see which would be the more careless in dress and Andrew was the winner. He was more stooped than a man of 42 should have been. He turned from the elevator door but either did not see or did not recognize Boyce. Boyce noted that his face was deeply lined and that the muscles in his neck were like ropes. His color was too red. Various people who kept in touch had told him that Andrew drank to excess, and he could see evidence of it. At last Boyce felt uncomfortable about his voyeurism and stepped forward. "Andrew," he said, extending his hand in greeting.

"Hello, Boyce," Andrew said as they shook hands but did not embrace. His voice sounded as tired and careworn as his face. "Good to see you again." He spoke English, but Boyce noticed that he sounded like someone who had never been to America, like a Korean who knew the language well but was unsure of correct pronunciation.

"Good to see you too," Boyce said. Embarrassed that he did not know what to say next he cleared his throat. "Are you hungry?"

"I can eat," Andrew said. "My treat."

"Oh no."

"Oh yes. Let's go." He led Boyce out to the street. "Sorry but the better places, where I usually take guests, are all closed this time on Sundays. They open only for dinner. It'll have to be a hash house."

"Fine by me."

They turned into a side alley and went into a modest but fairly clean diner. The menu was above the counter, and they both ordered the plate of the day. Boyce ordered barley water, and Andrew drank beer. It seemed to Boyce that he drank it with a great thirst. He finished the first bottle and ordered another. Only when they had finished eating and Andrew was drinking his second bottle did they take up the subject that was on their minds.

"Boyce, I know why you came back, after all this time," Andrew said. He belched and asked pardon. "But I hope you won't get involved. I think it's pretty obvious that Ji-wan was mixed up in the assassination. There's no way she will get off. All you'll do if you intervene is get yourself in trouble—and the church."

"I... feel an obligation—to Kim Ji-wan, to our parents, to the mission."

"Yes, I know, so do I. But I've made peace with the Regime Yi; and I have to live here. You can go back home, even if you're deported, but I can't. My business is here."

"It's going well?"

"What? Oh. Yes. Yes, very well." Andrew looked defensive. "I'll bet I make more each year than you do."

"I'm sure you do," Boyce laughed, hoping to reassure him, although by Andrew's appearance he very much doubted it.

"The church is not as divided about it as some say. There are a few radicals who would love to be martyrs, sure, emulate the early ones, but the vast majority says live and let live. They believe Ji-wan was a fool to get involved with the plot. They say leave well enough alone."

"What if our parents had said leave well enough alone? What if our grandparents had said leave well enough alone? What if they had gone home—or never come here to begin with?"

"Maybe they should have left. Maybe they shouldn't have come. Maybe you and I would both be better off. Maybe Korea would be. All this place cost them was distress and early death."

Andrew paid for the meal with small bills and walked Boyce back to his hotel. "Will you call me?" Boyce asked him.

"Sure I will," Andrew smiled sadly. "Brothers ought not to see each other only every quarter century." He started to walk away, then turned. He took a card out of his coat pocket and handed it to Boyce. It was wrinkled and soiled, but it bore Andrew Mann's name, the company he represented, and a telephone number. "You can all me there anytime," he said. They parted company at the hotel door.

A small man of nondescript appearance followed Boyce into the elevator and got out with him on his floor. As Boyce went down the hallway to his room the man hurried up to walk beside him and took his arm. "Keep walking," the man said. When Boyce looked alarmed, the man said, "Please don't be afraid. I am not a criminal." That did little to reassure Boyce, but he continued to walk with the man, passing his own door and going with him to the window at the end of the hall. There they stopped. He noticed that the rooms on both sides of the hall were storage closets. No one would hear them there.

"I am one of Ji-wan's people," the man whispered. "We have arranged for you to see her tomorrow morning."

"In the prison?" Boyce said.

"Yes. She cannot leave there."

"But... how did you manage it?"

"How? What do you mean how?"

"How did you get government approval? I assumed I would have to make a request to see her and that it would require official approval. I was prepared to wait a considerable time."

"We have... ways," the man said.

"Can I check to see that you are legitimate?"

"Check?"

"With official offices?"

"No," the man said firmly. "Not if you want to see her, don't do anything. Just let us take care of it. Be ready at 10:00 tomorrow. We will call you down to the lobby."

The man turned and headed down the hall. Boyce waited for him to disappear down a staircase, then made his way to his room and collapsed on the bed. He woke at five, in time to have a regularly scheduled meal in the hotel dining room. Then he tossed and turned all through the night.

6

kim ji-wan

Boyce woke every half hour through the night, wondering what the little man's visit meant, whether he would really get to see Kim Ji-Wan or was being suckered, perhaps in danger. Finally near daybreak he fell into a deep sleep and dreamed that he was buried in a leaky coffin, damp from water entering through cracks, with ants crawling over him. He woke with a start, wet with sweat despite a breeze that came through his open window. Thus the water. He heard noises, the normal sounds of a city waking but also hammering and shouting. He got up and went to the window and saw across the street workmen swarming over a building under construction. Thus the ants.

He felt nauseous and decided to skip breakfast. He went down the stairs, through the lobby, and into the street and mixed with the Monday morning crowds. He continued to be surprised at the crush of people. When he left Korea in 1948 it had a population of a six hundred thousand; now the number was eight million. He knew from correspondence that the city had grown—"everyone wants to live in Seoul, everyone leaves the village as soon as possible and comes to the city" more than one person had written—but he was unprepared for such an explosion.

School children were everywhere, walking to classes, taking city buses; and they looked identical. In order to encourage equality, President Yi said, all children should have the same hair styles and uniforms. Girls had to have their hair bobbed above the ears, boys had to have theirs buzzed. Both girls and boys had to wear identical black uniforms, girls with skirts and blouses, boys with pants and shirts. Neither girls nor boys could have any color in their garb.

Everyone was in a hurry, and because of the large numbers they constantly bumped into each other. The first several times this happened to Boyce, he expressed apologies to the person he jostled; but after a time he realized there was no need. No one seemed to notice the accidental confrontations, no one apologized, everyone took these bumps as part of the price of hurrying to work or to school.

The noises that had awakened him grew louder and more insistent. Fumes from buses assaulted his nose. He realized how spoiled he was to live in a small American city surrounded by forests, to teach at a school with vast open spaces, where the air was almost always sweet and he could always hear bird songs in the trees. He wondered what living in Seoul would have done to his ears and lungs, what it was doing to the ears and lungs of those who had lived through the population explosion and industrial revolution, both continuing apace, unchecked by any environmental laws. Move forward, with all speed, seemed to be Korea's slogan, to hell with the consequences.

He noticed two Korean girls, perhaps nineteen, certainly no longer in school, talking animatedly at the entrance to an alley; and the way they were dressed made him stop and pretend to window shop so that he could observe them more closely. They wore jeans and high heels and smoked cigarettes, everything designed to cheapen their natural Asian beauty. They talked so loudly—unlike proper Korean young ladies—that he could make out what they were saying. They spoke English, but it was what he had heard a linguist describe as Black English.

"He done promise me he'd take me home widdim," one said.

"You a fool, girl. He ain't gonna take you to no Amer'ca."

"What for not?"

"Cain't gitchu no veezza."

"He say he gonna take me to d'embassy 'n' tell 'em, 'Here dis girl, she pregna't, you gimme veezza, or I leave 'er here. Be yo problem."

Feeling sick, Boyd moved on. This was the price of American military aid.

When he returned to his hotel, three people were waiting for him in the lobby: the little man from yesterday with two other men, various sizes and shapes but just as nondescript as he. "Where have you been?" the little man said. "What are you late?"

Boyce glanced at the clock above the clerk's desk. It said 9:10. "You said around 9:00."

"I said 9:00. When Korean say 9:00 he mean 9:00. This not China."

"All right," Boyce said, irritated.

"Important to be on time to prison," the man said and led them out to the street, where a car was waiting. Boyce hesitated but then got in. It made him feel somewhat better to note that the desk clerk was standing at the hotel door watching them. He would be able to describe the car should Boyce not return at a reasonable hour.

The driver negotiated the heavy traffic like a race car competitor, with skill and abandon. Boyce stopped looking ahead after the third near miss. It took them only a half hour to make a trip that probably should have taken an hour. The prison was on the south edge of the city. Despite the natural beauty of the countryside around it, the barbed wire enclosed structure was dark, forbidding.

The others stayed in the car as the little man led Boyce to the front gate and spoke to the guard. The guard nodded and opened to let Boyce in. The little man remained outside. The guard led Boyce across a gravel yard and into the main building. He took him to a room, indicated a grouping of chairs, and left him there. After a ten minute wait, during which time Boyce grew ever more nervous, another door opened, and another guard brought a small woman in.

It took Boyce several anxious moments to recognize Ji-wan. She wore prison green overalls, which were too large for her and made her look smaller than he remembered her. Her hair was cut short, and she wore no makeup. She was thin, wan, and tired. She was now 44 years old, but she looked much older. She smiled sadly and came to Boyce. He embraced her and asked in English how she was. She merely nodded. "Good," she said in Korean.

The guard left the room and shut the door a bit too firmly behind him. Boyce was surprised at this. He thought such visits required an official presence. He led Ji-wan over to the chairs, and they sat down facing each other. "Now tell me truly," he repeated in English, "how are you?"

She looked all around the room, her eyes narrow, searching

for signs of listening devices, but then she shrugged as if it were a futile exercise. She replied to his question in English. "It's... it's been hard."

"I can imagine. I came as soon as they let me know."

"All the way from Carolina?"

"All the way from Italy."

"Italy," she said with a sigh. "That sounds nice."

"I'm glad I have the year off, to come and be here."

Her eyes cleared. "How... how has your life been, Boyce? I have had only rare snatches, from you, from others."

"It's been... I suppose easy is the best word. Easier than I deserved. Easy enough so that I feel guilty."

"Guilty?" The word seemed to disturb Ji-wan. "Guilty about what?"

"That I never returned, I suppose. I remained in school throughout the war here. I took a teaching job at a good school, where the demands on me were light. I... married."

"She died?"

"Yes."

"Children?"

"None."

"You did right, Boyce," she said. "Korea killed your dear parents, and it would have killed you. I was with them both when they died, did you know that?"

"No."

"I was having tea with your mother when the thugs broke into the house. They were searching for one of her guests. She refused to let them go past the foyer, and they shot her in the stomach. Then they ran away. I was in her room at the hospital when she died."

Tears welled up in Boyce's eyes and began to roll down his cheeks. Ji-wan reached out and brushed them away. "She loved you, Ji-wan," he said. "You were her little girl."

"Yes." She fought her own tears. "I stayed with your father in our mountain retreat for the year there, until he too died. Korea was the death of them both."

"Korea was their mission."

"Isn't it the same thing?"

Boyce looked about the room, then spoke quietly. "What about this case? The assassination. Why you?"

"I was not a part of the plot," she said firmly. "I am completely innocent of the charges against me. Not that it will matter. They've already decided that I will spend the rest of my life in prison—or worse. But I knew absolutely nothing about it."

"Then why?"

"It's complicated. I know too much about Yi. I know his attraction to young girls. He wanted me to provide him with lambs for shearing from my orphans and students, and I adamantly refused. Then I have spoken out against government oppression, especially when it interfered with church work. And I publicly defended the men arrested in the assassination. I did not say they were innocent, but I opposed their summary execution. Not that it did any good."

"So you are guilty by association."

"Not even that. I did not know the men."

"Why did you do all this? I understand refusing to be Yi's pimp, but why speak out against the government? Pastor Ju does not do this. The Catholic bishop does not. And why criticize the executions, if the men were probably guilty and you did not know them?"

"It is my duty as a Christian," she said simply. "I learned that from your parents. I have taken their cross."

"Are you afraid?"

"Of prison? No. Of execution?" She hesitated. "No." I have learned to live easily with danger. After that night, do you remember, when they were bombing, I was so afraid and nothing bad happened, that I have never been afraid again."

"That night... "

"I cherish it."

"I feel guilty about that too."

"Why?"

"At first guilty because I felt we had committed a sin. John Calvin would have said so."

"It was love, Boyce."

"My father would have said it was lust. He taught us never to touch a Korean girl, that if we did it would destroy the mission. I loved you, Ji-wan, and I swore that I would one day return and marry you. I feel guilty that I did not."

"No, you mustn't, Boyce. I have no regrets. I've been able to fulfill myself by going through life as an old maid." She smiled.

"You have become a celebrity."

"Yes. Not such a good thing, though, in a fascist dictatorship." She shook her head, as if to clear her mind. "Have you seen Andrew?"

"Yes. We shared a meal yesterday. He looks... "

"Derelict?"

"Yes."

"He never recovered from the loss of his mother and father. He never went abroad, never finished school. He doesn't work."

"He said he does imports. He showed me a card."

"It's fiction. He lives on the charity of the church. He even lives in one of our houses. Pastor Ju doesn't have the temerity to put him out."

"Can I help? Would he let me?"

"No. He's too proud. Missionary royalty, you know. No, you just have to let him alone, let him drink himself to death."

"Can I help you?"

Ji-wan's eyes swept the room again. She spoke in a whisper. "You must be careful. As an American you would not be imprisoned, but you might be deported without warning. My people have contacted you, and they will do so again. Do as they say. But even then be wary. We suspect spies have even infiltrated our group. Trust no one absolutely. There... "

Both doors opened abruptly, simultaneously, and a guard entered by both. Ji-wan stood. "It's time for me to go," she said.

Boyce stood and nodded.

"Please. Be careful," Ji-wan said. She took his hand and pressed it. Then she turned and followed the guard, who stood at the door and ushered her into the cell blocks.

Boyce walked over and followed the other guard. The man led him out into the courtyard and to the front gate. Outside there was no car waiting. Boyce walked several blocks until he came to a thoroughfare, then took a cab to his hotel. It had all taken only a little more than an hour.

At four o'clock all three channels on Boyce's television set broadcast the same program, a documentary in praise of Yi Dong-ho and his vast achievements for the people of Korea. It showed film clips of his career as a military officer and as president. In snippets from his speeches he told his version of what made his Korea great. Boyce, who knew the true story, found himself juxtaposing the façade with the reality.

Yi portrayed himself as the complete, thorough, unadulterated Korean leader, uncontaminated by foreign or communist influences. Boyce knew that as a young man he had been an officer in the Japanese army, trained by that fascist regime; and he knew that at one time between the end of World War II and the Korean War he had made himself available to serve the communist government in the north. Only in mid life had he become an anti-communist, anti-Japanese thoroughly Korean patriot.

Yi said that the society he was in the process of recovering and building was based on the moral principles of Confucius. Having heard from Ji-wan about Yi's weakness for young girls, Boyce wondered where in the writings of Confucius Yi found pedophilia to be a virtue.

Yi said that his government was a bulwark against communism is Asia and that the capitalist nations of Europe and North America would always stand behind him and his defense of their economic systems. Boyce wondered if Koreans knew that most European nations were socialist, and he wondered how capitalistic Yi's nationalization of the Korean banking system was.

Yi said that he would guarantee that democracy reigned supreme in the Land of the Morning Calm. Boyce ticked off in his mind the erosion of human rights in the country: speech, press, assembly, religion. He thought of George Orwell and how in *1984* white was black and black was white. Under Yi fascism was democracy.

As martial music grew louder, the camera pulled back from Yi so that he could come out from behind a podium and accept the applause of his audience. A young Korean lady, dressed in traditional garb, came up to take a bow with him. Boyce knew this was Yi's eldest daughter, who at the age of 24, upon the death of her mother, had taken on the duties of First Lady of Korea. She was all smiles, while her father was grim. Hers was the perfect look and personality of a fine Korean lady.

Yet Boyce had learned during the hour's program to be suspicious, to mistrust everything; and so he wondered what lies the picture of the brave president and his bubbly daughter covered. He wondered whether Yi fully trusted his daughter with her role, whether she was as devoted to him and to the nation as she seemed, whether she were as healthy of body and mind as she pretended to be, whether the gunmen who killed Yi's wife had missed their target or actually hit it. He wondered if Yi had orchestrated his own wife's death in order to be rid of her, in order to have freedom to pursue his little girls, in order to create pity and support from his oppressed people.

Boyce realized he had become a cynic.

7

the dead

On Tuesday morning, having seen no more of the little man who took him to the prison or either of the other two men, Boyce decided it was time for him to visit the cemetery on Missionary Ridge. He had not had time before this. He took a long shower and lingered over his hotel breakfast, dreading the trip he knew he had to make. It was not until after 11:00 that he caught a taxi and gave the driver instructions. Because of the heavy traffic, because the driver was not familiar with the part of the city he indicated, and because the city had changed so much that Boyce could offer him little help, they were lost several times; and it was almost noon before he emerged from the cab at the big Iron Gate.

The cemetery was smaller than he remembered it, closed in now by urban sprawl. He could no longer see the river from the grounds as he remembered he had once been able to do; but he could smell it as he could not remember being able to do when it was still uncontaminated. The Iron Gate was more modest than he remembered it, less ornate. It was not locked and yielded easily to his push, and he walked onto the holy ground.

What had once seemed unlimited space for new graves was now completely filled. Many foreigners had died in Seoul since 1885. Boyce knew where his grandparents were buried, and he picked his way through the stones, around to the left, until he found them. Their stones were greatly weathered, but their names, their dates of birth and death, and comforting scripture verse for each were clearly visible. His eyes moved up and above those stones to two newer ones, and he walked up a rise to visit his parents. He had never been to their graves.

Their stones bore names and dates and scripture verses like those of the older couple; but near the bottom of each was a bit of poetry. On his mother's were the words "she kept watch over the bitter sweet kettles of life," and on his father's were the words, "he guarded the ramparts with a velvet sword." Boyce wondered who had composed such words, whether they were original or taken from a book. He couldn't remember having seen them anywhere before. He had never known Andrew to do any composition. Ji-wan?

He stood for a long, lost time staring at the stones, trying to make sense of the fact that his parents were indeed gone. All these years, as he lived his life in America, because he was not here to bury them, he always felt they were still alive, at their home in Korea, and that he would someday return here and see them again, talk with them, share with them memories of his childhood. Now facing these cold hard stones he knew the truth: they were gone, completely, and he would never see them again, not on this earth, beyond this earth only if their faith in the life eternal proved to be true.

He was unaware that three people had come up behind him until one of them spoke. Boyce turned. It was the little man who took Boyce to the prison but did not bring him back. With him was a taller, heavier man and a small but formidable woman but not the two from the day before. The little man said, "We are Ji-wan's people," and the other two nodded in affirmation. All three looked furtively around the grave yard as they talked. Boyce kept his eyes fixed on the three of them. The conversation was in Korean.

"How did you find me?" Boyce asked.

"We followed you from the hotel," the little man explained. "Your driver was not very efficient."

"What do you want?"

"We need your help," the woman said. "We have a plan, and you are a key part of it. We must get Ji-wan out of the country."

"If we do not," the taller man said, "she will be executed."

"She told me she is innocent, that she had nothing to do with the assassination, and just for speaking out in defense of the accused she can go to jail but not be executed."

"She is not innocent," the little man said. "She told you that because she knew the room was bugged; but she was a part of the plot. It all went wrong, and Mrs. Yi was killed, not president, the intended target."

"Ji-wan took part in a plot to murder the president?"

"Yes."

"But... " Boyce was stunned. "But murder is a sin. It breaks one of the Ten Commandments. Thou shalt not kill."

"Have you heard of Dietrich Bonheoffer, Dr. Mann?" the taller man said.

Boyce was surprised to hear a Korean mention Bonheoffer, the Lutheran pastor who joined a plot to assassinate Hitler toward the end of World War II. "I have heard of him," Boyce said. "He believed Hitler was so evil that killing him was not against God's commandments."

"So believes Ji-wan about Yi," the woman said.

"He has robbed us of our freedom," the little man said.

"You are free to preach the Gospel."

"Only if we do not preach against corruption," the tall man said. "Only if we do not preach the whole Gospel."

"Bonheoffer was executed."

"So will be Ji-wan," the tall man said.

A thought crossed Boyce's mind and caused his throat to tighten. "Is... was my brother involved? Is he in danger?"

"Your brother?" the woman said, then she laughed. "No, he's harmless, everyone knows that. He is a sycophant."

"You are the one we turn to," the little man said. "You are the one who can help us now."

"Help you how?"

The three Koreans came closer to Boyce and formed a tight circle around him. He couldn't imagine that anyone would be able to hear them here in the middle of the cemetery, but the trio seemed not so sure. The tall man spoke: "We have contacts with... certain people... in Japanese Embassy. They are willing to help us. There will be a boat... We also have friends in the American Embassy who will... make arrangements for you... to meet the president."

"The president?" Boyce said, frowning. "Yi?"

"Yes."

"How? Why?"

"He listens to the Americans," the woman said. "Without them he would be vulnerable to Northern attack. They will tell him who you are, that as a courtesy he should invite you for a meeting. He will obey. You will go to visit him, the photographers will take publicity shots—you the son and grandson of the great Protestant Mission, smiling benevolently on the current head of state, giving your approval to him—you must pretend to approve so that he will not suspect why you are here—and the reason you are there, while you talk with him, is to find out for us when Ji-wan's trial is to take place."

"Why is that important?" Boyce said.

The tall man moved even closer to Boyce. "If we know when she is to be moved from prison to the court, we can make definite plans to take her from the authorities and get her safely out of the country."

"How am I supposed to find this out?"

"We are trusting you to do it, in whatever way you can."

"Who are these friends of yours in the Japanese and American Embassies?" Boyce said.

The small man answered. "The less you know the better."

"Yes, but I... "

The tall man held a forefinger to his lips. "Shhh," he said.

The three looked around them and walked away, in different directions, and were soon out of the Iron Gate and gone.

Boyce waited for some time before he said farewells to the stones, to the dead Manns who had given their lives to Korea and now rested in her soil. When he emerged from the cemetery he looked in every direction for spies, since Ji-wan had warned him to beware of them, but saw no one. He had to walk a mile or more to find a thoroughfare and a taxi to take him to his hotel.

He wanted desperately to talk with Andrew; but from what everyone said, and from his own observations, Andrew was not to be trusted. He had accepted the status quo, adapted to the circumstances, let himself be used, depended on the good will of those who did not want controversy. All Boyce would do by bringing him into this cabal was put him in danger.

When he arrived at his hotel the desk clerk, with a knowing look, handed him two messages, from two callers, asking him to respond. One was from the American Embassy, the other from the Blue House. He went to his room and freshened up before he made the calls.

"Embassy of the United States," a voice said in English, then repeated in Korean. No discernible accent in either language, but Boyce guessed the woman was Korean. Koreans seemed better able to imitate the American speech than Americans to imitate Korean.

"This is Boyce Mann. I had a message to call for a... Mister Samuels?"

"One moment please," she said. There was a silence, and then a man, obviously American, came on. "Dr. Boyce. So good of you to return my call so quickly. "Ed Samuels here."

"Yes?" Boyce wondered whether Samuels did not know his family name or was trying to be familiar. Either way he was mildly offended.

"Dr. Boyce, I would like to extend to you an official invitation, from the Ambassador, to attend a reception in your honor at his residence on Friday night at 6:00 p.m." It sounded like the man was reading from a card, which Boyce thought probable. "Would you be able to come?"

"I think so," Boyce said. "I only have my regular professorial suit."

"That will be fine. The Ambassador prefers things to be kept fairly casual. Great. We'll look for you. Thanks, Dr. Boyce."

"Yes. Thank you."

Boyce sat looking at the telephone. A reception, in his honor, for what purpose? Ji-wan's people had promised to arrange a meeting with Park, but they had said nothing about an invitation from the American Embassy. They had said the Americans would help them, and so maybe this was a part of the plot. He felt sweat on his forehead. He dreaded making the second call, but after a time he sighed and dialed the number.

"Hello. What is your business?" came a man's voice, deep and authoritative, speaking Korean.

"My name is Boyce Mann," Boyce said in Korean. "I was asked to call this number."

There was a long silence. "Yes, Doctor Mann," the voice said. "I have instructions to invite you to come to the Blue House, to meet with President Yi, at fifteen hundred hours on Wednesday. You will come?" The last sentence was phrased as a question, but its tone left no doubt that the answer was to be yes.

"I will come," Boyce said.

"Thank you, sir. Wednesday at fifteen hundred. Goodbye."

Boyce listened to the dial tone for a time before he replaced the receiver. So Ji-wan's people had made their arrangements. He was now an actor in a drama whose plot he knew only in vague outline. He was given no lines, just broad stage directions. The curtain was rising.

8

the man

Boyce slept badly once more, and after 4:00 he never got back to sleep. He was up and dressed by 7:00, with nothing to do. After breakfast he stood for a long time staring out at the men working on the new building across the street. He had noticed that they never left the site, eating, sleeping, and he supposed eliminating without coming down for a break. Apparently their contract called for continuing their work without interruption until it was completed, either that or they were paid by the hour and couldn't afford to lose hours traveling to and from home. He wondered whether they were married, had children, had families; and then it occurred to him that they were country men, living in Seoul because there were jobs there, saving every cent to take back with them for dependents on the farm. He wondered where this mad dash to build and modernize would end—or if it ever would.

He managed somehow to pass the morning and noon time and arrived at the Blue House, Korea's presidential residence, just before 3:00, or as President Park's military minded assistants called it 1500 hours. He gave his name to the guard at the gate, the guard made a telephone call, and with swift precision a young Korean man in a blue suit came to meet him and ushered him through the gate, across a courtyard lined with limousines parked in regimental order, and into the mansion.

In the foyer Boyce noticed several Korean women, all young, all quite pretty, hurrying around, looking efficient and busy. Amid this array of feminine charm he saw coming toward him another young Korean man in another blue suit and an American, a bit older, in a grey suit. They both offered hands and names—Shu and Eriksen—and welcomed Boyce to the president's home. "Come this way," Eriksen said. The guide who had brought him this far faded away, and the two men led him through an ornate doorway into a small office furnished with plush chairs. Shu indicated one for Boyce, and the two of them sat opposite him. Eriksen did the talking. Boyce identified the accent as somewhere west of Chicago. There was just a touch of Scandinavian exaggeration.

"Doctor Mann," Eriksen said, "I am political attaché at the U.S. Embassy. Mr. Shu is political adviser to President Yi." Shu nodded. "We are both very happy that you have returned to Korea, your birthplace I'm told, and that you have accepted the president's invitation to see him this afternoon." Eriksen cleared his throat and frowned. "Your family is still beloved here, and we believe you can have a strong positive influence on... circumstances in Seoul."

"Perhaps," Boyce said carefully.

Eriksen crossed his legs, in an effort to appear calm, but a twitch in his left eye betrayed nervousness. "We just wanted to offer a few constructive suggestions about your meeting with President Yi."

"Oh?"

"Yes. As you know the president highly values his relations with the United States; and he is anxious to recognize Americans who have made contributions to the national development and welfare of Korea. This is why he wants to meet you. This is why your meeting should be without, shall we say, any thorns among the roses."

Boyce thought this was an odd turn of phrase, but he did not reply. He simply waited for Andrews to go on.

"You should discuss freely your family's history in the country; and you should answer any questions he asks, answer truthfully of course, but make an effort not to introduce topics that are controversial, topics he cannot discuss openly, topics that might embarrass him."

"Such as... "

"Well, we know, for example, that you hold one of the assassination conspirators in strong regard."

"Kim Ji-wan."

"Uh, yes. You knew her when you were both children."

"Yes, for many years, until I went away to university."

"Yes. Well, any mention of the assassination attempt is very unsettling to the president. You know that his wife was killed."

"I do."

"You know that he has taken no part in the investigation or in the arrests; and so he cannot comment on the case. Thus it is best for you not to raise the issue with him."

"Why would I?"

"Oh, you wouldn't, I'm sure. We just wanted to make it clear that this topic is off the table." Eriksen uncrossed and recrossed his legs. His left eye twitched again. "Things are about to take a turn for the better in Korea. Our ambassador meets regularly with the president, always gently encouraging him to liberalize his administration; and we feel certain this is paying off. We may well be close to a major shift in policy."

"Civil rights might be restored?"

"Please, Doctor Mann," Eriksen said, uncrossing his legs, sitting forward in his chair. "It is best not to talk about civil rights, whether they might be restored, because that implies they have been curtailed. Do you understand?"

Boyce smiled. "Yes, Mr. Eriksen, I think I understand."

"Then you will be most cautious in your choice of words, you will talk only about the things the president brings to your attention."

"I understand."

Eriksen was still not satisfied. He glanced at Shu. Shu was impassive. Eriksen sighed and smiled. "Good. Good. Then it is time for us to go into the president's private rooms."

He got up, Shu followed suit, and the three of them went back into the foyer, past the bevy of beautiful young women, and down a hallway. An armed guard standing by a door saluted them, knocked lightly on the door, then opened it to admit the three. The guard bowed out and closed the door behind him.

Boyce could see in the darkened room a large desk with a smallish man behind it. To the man's left stood an armed guard in uniform, and to his right stood a beautiful girl in a silk dress slit up the side to her hip. Without saying a word, the man beckoned for them to come toward him. As they neared the desk, Shu bowed deeply and Eriksen dipped his head in a show of respect. Boyce merely nodded. The guard came around the desk and signaled where each was to sit, Boyce in the middle chair directly in front of Yi and Shu and Eriksen on either side of him. Boyce noted as they sat that both Shu and Eriksen crossed their hands in their laps to hide their nervous quavers.

"Professor Mann," Yi Dong-ho said with a smile. "I am glad at long last to meet you. I have heard much about you." He spoke English with a heavy accent. Boyce detected in the accent both a Korean and a Japanese influence. He thought once again about how Yi had been an officer in the Japanese army.

"Thank you, sir," Boyce said in Korean. "I am glad also to meet you. I have heard much about you as well."

Yi smiled and seemed to relax. "You speak Korean. You speak it very well," he said in Korean. Even his Korean had a faintly Japanese sound.

"Yes, I spoke more Korean than English until I was eighteen."

"When you went away to school."

"Yes sir."

"And you never returned, not until now."

Boyce could not decide whether it was a mere comment or a reprimand. He did not answer.

"Would you like tea?" Yi said. Without waiting for a reply, he signaled the girl at his side, she went quickly to a sideboard and poured four cups and brought them to Yi and his three guests. All four men took a sip. "Do you like it?" Yi asked. "Do you know what it is?"

"It is ginseng, is it not?" Eriksen said in a heavily accented Korean.

"That is right," Yi said. "It is good for a man. It increases his powers."

Eriksen nodded with a smile as Shu blushed. Boyce, who knew the superstition that ginseng was an aphrodisiac, merely took another sip.

....

93 • thomas woods

"I also eat snake soup," Yi said with a quick laugh. "It is also good for a man, it also increases his powers."

Boyce looked at the young lady, but her eyes were on the floor.

"Who will win your election?" Yi asked Boyce.

"The presidential election? It's probably too early to tell. The incumbent usually has an advantage, but with the Nixon fiasco, President Ford is in trouble. He is being challenged by the actor Ronald Reagan; and then we don't yet know who the Democrats will nominate. Governor Carter is doing surprisingly well in some of the early caucuses."

"Carter, no," Yi said. "He is a weak man, too religious. I admire religious people, in their place, in the church, in the temple, but not in politics. You need a strong president who will do whatever it takes to resist and defeat the communist menace, not one who asks whether an action is moral or immoral. I have read Machiavelli, I have studied Bismarck. They knew about politics. Jesus and Confucius knew about religion and ethics, but not about politics."

"You can separate the two?" Boyce said.

Eriksen darted Boyce a warning glance.

"Oh yes," Yi said. "Separation of church and state. That is a good old American principle, is it not? Church in its place, not interfering with state, and state in its place, not interfering with church."

"Who is your choice in the election?" Boyce asked.

Again Eriksen gave him a warning look.

"Me?" Yi smiled. "I cannot vote. I express no opinion, not publicly. I must work with the American people's choice. I like President Ford very much. He and I are both pragmatic. Governor

Carter is an idealist. An idealistic peanut farmer." Yi laughed, and Eriksen and Shu joined in the laughter.

"But Doctor Mann," Yi went on after another sip of his tea. "You have been away many years, and so you can see Korea with fresh eyes. What do you notice? How do you find the nation?"

"It has certainly changed," Boyce said.

"Yes. For the better I hope."

"Yes, for the better." Boyce saw Eriksen relax. "Like a cultivated pearl, a pearl with only one flaw." He saw Eriksen tense up again. "The world sees Korea as an amazing example of economic and social progress. The world also sees that in the area of civil rights Korea has not made such progress."

Eriksen started to speak up, but Yi held up a warning hand. He signaled for Boyce to go on.

"I am here, as you know, because of my dear friend Kim Ji-wan. You could add to Korea's positive image in the world immensely if you released her." Eriksen started to speak, but Boyce put a hand on his arm. "Perhaps if she poses a threat to peace she could be sent into permanent exile."

Yi was obviously angered by Boyce's audacity, but he showed admirable restraint. He held his temper. He was silent for a long time, staring at Boyce, and when he spoke it was with a firm voice.

"Such would be a sign of weakness," he said. "If I am lenient with one criminal, other criminals will take heart, and there will be chaos. As you know, I ended the chaos of our politics when I took office in 1961. I am all that stands between the Republic of Korea and a mad man. Kim Il-sung is crazy. He would start a civil war even more bloody than the one a quarter of a century ago."

"Kim Ji-wan has said... " Boyce did not want to mention his visit, although he knew Park doubtlessly was aware of it. "...that her only crime is testifying to her Christian faith."

Yi answered with a soft voice but also a bitter tone. "Doctor Boyce, my daughter is a Christian, did you know that?"

"Yes sir."

"She is very religious. And my dear departed wife was a Buddhist, just as religious in her way as my daughter is in hers. Were the men who killed her testifying to their Christian faith?"

"No sir. The attempted assassination was a criminal act, contrary to the teachings of Jesus."

"Exactly. And Kim Ji-wan helped plan their criminal act."

"I don't believe that is true," Boyce said. "With all respect."

"Then I suppose we must disagree," Yi said calmly. He cleared his throat and leaned forward. "But I do need your help, doctor. That is why I asked you to come here today. There could be great disorder in the churches when the court's judgment is carried out. I would like you to use the great prestige of your family's name to encourage calm."

"Not even a peaceful protest?"

"There is no such thing among Koreans, doctor. You know that. Protest always leads to violence, violence to chaos, chaos to communism." He looked Boyce in the eyes. "You cannot save Kim Ji-wan. You *can* save the lives of a multitude of Korean Christians. You can preach peace."

Boyce thought about his mission, the request Kim Ji-wan's people made of him. "Sir, would you permit me to be present at her trial? I would remain silent, I would not interfere. I want to be able to give her support in her hour of need."

Yi was silent for a long time. The two men on either side of Boyce squirmed in their chairs. At last he nodded. "I can do that. In exchange for your promise to preach peace."

"Yes sir. That I will promise."

"The trial will be next Monday," Yi said. "I will send a driver to the Chosun Hotel for you. You will pardon me if I do not tell you where the trial will be conducted. It is a sensitive event and cannot be held in the public eye. But you may be present. The driver will bring you."

"Thank you, sir."

"Now," Yi said, standing up. "We must have an official, historical record of your visit, of Korea's president meeting for the first time the scion of the famous missionary family." He nodded to the pretty girl, and she went to a side door and brought in a photographer. Yi came out from behind his desk and took his place between Boyce and Eriksen, with Shu beside Eriksen. The photographer urged them to smile and snapped several pictures. Then Yi turned and offered his hand to Boyce, the two other men faded away, and the photographer snapped several pictures of the two men shaking hands, smiling at each other.

At last Yi nodded to the photographer that he had taken enough pictures and let go Boyce's hand. "Thank you very much, Doctor," he said formally. He nodded to the armed guard, and the guard signaled for the three men to follow him. All three bowed to Yi in various degrees of obsequiousness and walked with the guard to the door. He led them out and turned them over to the guard in the hall way. As they walked toward the foyer Eriksen whispered, "What in hell did you do that for?"

"Do what?" Boyce said.

"You showed your ass big and white," Eriksen hissed. "Who knows what you've stirred up? Damn, oh damn it to hell."

Before Boyce could reply a messenger touched him on the arm. "Doctor Boyce Mann?" the man in still another blue suit asked.

"Yes."

"It is request that you wait here for a moment." He spoke to the guard. "Take these other two men out."

Shu looked frightened, Eriksen angry. They both followed orders and let the guard take them away.

"Now, you will please follow me," the man said.

"What is it?" Boyce demanded.

"Over here," he man said, beckoning Boyce to follow him to an alcove in the hallway. When they were apparently out of sight and hearing, he whispered, "Miss Yi will see you."

"Miss Yi?"

"President daughter."

"She will see me? Now?"

"No, not at present. You will come to her residence... " He handed Boyce a card with an address on it. "... at 2:00 on tomorrow afternoon."

"Well, I... "

"You will come," the man said. "She will see you."

The man walked away, down the hall, toward the door to the foyer. Boyce followed him. The man opened the door and let him out. There a guard led him to the front door and opened it for him. Out in the courtyard he saw no sign of Eriksen or Shu. He walked to the gate and was ushered out into the street.

He stood there for a long time, thinking about what had happened to him, the briefing about what not to say, the official interview during which he had obviously said things he should not have said, the staged photographs, the surreptitious message about tomorrow. It was almost too much to digest at one time. He decided rather than take a taxi to walk the mile or so back to his hotel.

As he passed one of the large new department stores, someone touched his arm, more than the usual brush of the crowd, and he felt pulled to the window. "Just pretend you are observing the merchandise," a voice said. He looked from side to side and saw the three people from the cemetery, the ones who called themselves Ji-wan's People.

"What did you find out?" the tall man asked. Boyce turned to him. "Keep looking in the window," he warned.

Boyce spoke without looking at the man. "The trial is Monday."

"Good," the smaller man said. "That confirms what we have been told."

Boyce wondered how many sources the group had. "Yi gave me permission to attend."

"Good," the woman said. "But of course that will not be possible if we are successful. We will take her from them when she is transferred from prison to the court."

"You don't know where the trial will be held," Boyce said. "He said it was top secret. I won't know until I am taken there."

"We don't need to know that," the taller man said. "We only need to know when she will leave the prison. And that will be Saturday morning."

"Why Saturday?" Boyce said. "The trial is on Monday."

"Yi is superstitious, he never does anything important to him on a Sunday. He is not a Christian, but he honors Sundays."

"Be prepared on Saturday morning, very early, we will pick you up outside your hotel."

"Me? Where am I going then?"

"You will see."

Boyce cleared his throat. "Let me mention this. A messenger told me as I was leaving that Miss Yi, the president's daughter, wishes to see me tomorrow afternoon."

"That is not surprising," the woman said.

"Why?"

"She is like her father. She likes variety. She has chosen you. To avoid suspicion, you must go. But be very careful. Don't mention us. Don't give the plot away."

Before Boyce could reply the three conspirators melted away and were absorbed by the crowds rushing down the street. Boyce walked on, lost in thought, bewildered, suspecting bad things, expecting the worst.

9

the woman

Boyce read the address from the card to the taxi driver who picked him up outside his hotel. The driver turned and gave Boyce a long look of disbelief, but Boyce nodded and told him in Korean that he had heard right. The driver shrugged and drove away. The ride took thirty minutes, but it would have taken half the time without the heavy mid day traffic.

He was taken to a large, old fashioned residence, one obviously built for a Japanese official probably in the 1920s, now remodeled and upgraded for the use of an important Korean official. "First Lady House," the driver said, pointing to the front gate, with its two uniformed armed guards.

"Yes. Thank you," Boyce said. He drove quickly away.

Boyce walked slowly to the gate and gave one of the guards his name. The guard saluted briskly and opened the gate. He led Boyce to the front door of the house and admitted him. There a man servant bowed to him and led him to a large back room, closed the door behind him, and left Boyce alone. The room had a desk with every available technical facility; but to one side there was also a king sized bed. Boyce wondered why an office and a bedroom were combined.

He stood in the middle of the room until a tiny servant girl came from a side door and offered him a cup of tea, then bowed and left him again. Boyce sniffed, then took a sip. Once more it was ginseng.

After another wait, while he drank the tea, the same side door opened and Miss Yi entered. He recognized her face, but from the neck down she looked quite different from her pictures in the newspapers. Those pictures showed her greeting the wives of foreign dignitaries, and in them she always wore traditional Korean garb. There she looked like a middle aged China doll. In the leisure suit she was slimmer and more petite and much younger than she appeared in the pictures. Boyce was surprised at how western she looked. He was also surprised to see that she was barefoot.

She came forward and offered her hand. "Professor Mann," she said in flawless English, with almost no accent, her voice low and soft, "I have long wanted to meet you."

"And I you," Boyce said. He spoke English as she did, assuming that she preferred it. Many educated Koreans did, the way Russians in the nineteenth century preferred to speak French.

"Did you enjoy your tea?" she asked him, noting that his cup was empty.

"Oh. Yes, thank you."

She took the cup and encouraged him to take a seat in an outsized leather easy chair. She placed the empty cup on her desk and took an identical leather chair facing him. "I am happy you could visit me at my residence," she said with a smile. "I know it was on short notice."

"Not at all," Boyce said. "I have quite a bit of time on my hands." He laughed, and she smiled in response. Not waiting for her to say more, he swept a hand over the room. "I am pleased to come here. It's a very nice place, this office, this entire house in fact."

"Yes," she said. "It was my mother's. She was First Lady, you know. She is dead. Villains killed her. Now I am filling her role."

"So I'm told. No one has a bad thing to say about you and the work you do. You are much admired."

"Thank you. As I always say, I can fill her role, but I can never fill her shoes. She was a remarkable woman."

The First Lady has a separate residence from the President?"

"Oh yes. This is traditional. The king and queen always had separate residences. My mother and father did. Now he and I do."

"I see."

"My father is the new king."

"Yes?"

"Of course we are no longer a kingdom, we are a republic." She smiled. "I don't know if you aware of this, but in fact there is still a king. He does not wear a crown, and he plays no part in our government. He lives quietly, in retirement, and does not interfere. His passion is gardening. Koreans do not want him to be their king, but in their hearts they miss having one. My father understands that, and he combines the political office of president with the spiritual office of king."

"I see."

"He has dedicated his life to the nation. I have missed having him spend time with me, but I know he has a higher calling."

"Oh."

She smiled. "Enough about the Yi's. I have read about your family. They are a vital part of our history and culture. They brought Christianity to us. For that I am grateful. You may know that I too am a Christian."

"Yes, I do know that."

"I enjoy so much talking with men of religion."

"Well," Boyce demurred. "I am not really a man of religion."

She smiled. A twinkle appeared in her eye. "I feel that you are. I feel you have a certain aura, almost a halo about your head, a light emanating from your body. I have psychic powers, spiritual vision. I can see such things in people. I have known several men with your aura, but it is rare." She turned her head to one side. "Father, will you do something for me? Will you grant me a special favor, Father?"

"If I can of course. But please, I am not a minister, and even if I were, we Protestants do not call... "

She held up a hand to stop him, got up, went to her desk, picked up a book, and brought it to Boyce. She held it so that he could see it was an English Bible. "Will you read to me?"

"Read to you?"

"Yes. As my priest did for me when I was a girl. He is gone now, gone to heaven, to his reward, and I miss him greatly. Having a man of faith read to me is so comforting, especially in these trying times."

"Well... " Boyce had no idea what this all meant, but he was faced with an emotional plea that he found hard to deny. She looked at him with pleading eyes, like a helpless child.

She held the book out toward him. It opened without coaxing to a certain page. "Here, she said, handing it to Boyce, "please read this." He took the book and noted from the page heading that it had opened on *The Song of Solomon*. "My priest often read it to me. Read the parts he marked. I love them so much. Please." She sat in her chair.

Boyce flipped through the few pages of the short work. Certain passages were set off in ink with brackets. He remembered from his childhood Bible classes that *The Song of Solomon* was an erotic poem written for use in King Solomon's bedroom, sensual enough to enable him service his multitude of wives. Boyce had always found it an embarrassment and wondered how it found its way into the Bible of his Puritan ancestors. The boys in his Bible classes found it hard not to snicker when it was read. He looked up and saw that she sat on the edge of his seat, eagerly waiting for him to begin.

"Oh that you would touch my mouth with the kisses of your lips! For your love is better than wine, your affection richer than the heaviest scented oil."

He stopped when she stood up, and he watched in utter amazement as she began to remove her suit. She wore nothing beneath it. "Go on, please go on," she said breathlessly as she dropped first her top and then her bottom to the floor and stood before him naked. He followed her command, stumbling over words but continuing as best he could, keeping his eyes on the text.

"You are beautiful, my love. Your eyes are doves, your teeth are ewes, your breasts are fawns , and your lips are scarlet threads..."

Boyce stopped as she came and slipped into his lap. She crossed her legs over his and laid her head against his chest.

"I... "

"Just read, just read to me, Father."

"But I'm not... "

"Read, Father, read."

He stumbled on. "You ravish my heart with a glance of your eyes. How sweet is your love, my bride, it is wine, it is oil, it is nectar."

She sat in his lap like a child. She hummed with pleasure. She put her thumb in her mouth and sucked it avidly. "You are near the end. Please finish, Father, finish," she said with a lisp. Her voice was husky.

"Come, my beloved, let us go forth into the fields and lodge in the villages. Let us go out early to the vineyards and see if the grape blossoms have opened. There I will give you my love."

"Yes," she said. "Give me your love, Father, give me your love." She hugged him tightly, her body growing taut. "Give me your love, give me your love. Oh Father, oh Father, I love you, my dear love, my dear, dear Father."

Boyce was ashamed to find himself tumescent, to realize that her ecstasy stimulated him so. She held him with strong arms for a long moment, then cried out, and relaxed with a great sigh. "Oh, Father, my lovely, lovely Father," she whispered as she licked his ear. Boyce felt damp warmth on his leg, too much to be only his flow. He realized that they had experienced simultaneous orgasm. He was immediately embarrassed and ashamed.

He listened, fully alert, as her breathing evened, and by the way she relaxed he knew she was asleep. He waited for a good half hour. At last she roused, yawned, and stretched. Her breasts bobbed against him. She drew away and looked him in the eyes.

"Forgive me, Father. Do you forgive me? I know I'm a bad girl, Father, but I can't help myself. God has made me the way I am, Father. Do you forgive me for my bad girl ways?"

Boyce nodded.

"Thank you, Father, thank you so much. It is not a sin if you forgive me. You have always been so good that way. You are a saint."

She slowly got up from his lap and quickly slipped back into her clothes. She took his hands and told him to stand, and as he did so he realized how shaken he was. His knees were weak and he stumbled. She quickly embraced and steadied him. She kissed him on the lips. "I must go now," she said. "But I will have you come again." She made sure he could stand alone. "I love you, Father, I love you." She turned and left the room.

Boyce did not move until the little servant girl reappeared, her eyes averted, and led him to the outer door. There she gave him over to the armed guard, who without a word or even a glance in his direction led him out of the residence and through the front gate. Boyce was on the street before he realized he had kept the Bible.

He was half way back to his hotel, on a street that led to Nam dae Mun, the ancient south gate of the old city, when he realized the three conspirators were walking on either side and behind him. "Here," the short man at his right side said, "go in here, pretend you are hungry." He indicated a noodle shop. Boyce went in with them. "Go on through the kitchen," the man whispered. They went through to a room at the back of the building. "What happened?" the taller man asked him. "In her house."

Boyce shrugged. "I'd rather not go into it. I met her."

"What is that book?" the woman asked.

Boyce had almost forgotten about the Bible. He held it up for them to see, and they all exchanged glances.

"It is hers?"

"Yes."

"Were you her father?"

"What do you know about that?"

"We all know," the woman said.

Boyce was embarrassed. How much did they know? How detailed, how widespread was the gossip about the First Lady? Embarrassment, as always, made him angry. He lashed out. "No more questions. I have done your bidding. I have given you the information you needed. Now I make a demand."

"Demand?"

"Yes. I'm going to help with Ji-wan's escape."

All three of them backed away. "No," they said in unison.

"Yes," Boyce said, his anger growing.

"But... it is very dangerous. You might be killed. Even if you are not, you will be seen, you will be implicated, and we cannot afford for that to happen. We need to keep you pure; you will be helpful to us in the future."

"I don't care what you need or want," Boyce said firmly. "I'm going along. How can I be sure you are who you say you are? How do I know you don't work for Yi, that this is some convoluted scheme, that you are planning to kill Ji-wan during the abduction, to avoid a trial?"

"If that were so," the tall man said, "why did we need you to tell us when she was being moved? Our ignorance proves that we are not with the regime."

"All right, let's assume you are what you claim, that you are Christians hoping to free Ji-wan. She might still be killed in the escape attempt. If not, you will whisk her away out of the country and never let it be known where she is. Either way I will not see her again."

"You will see her again—in another country. We will not fail."

"How can I be sure?" He spoke slowly, firmly. "Here is what we will do. I will tell the hotel clerk that I am hiring a car to take me to the countryside, to visit old friends of my family. One of you will come for me, pretending to be the driver of the car I've hired. How many will be in the plot, how many people?"

"Twelve. Four in three cars."

"All right. My car follows the other three. If you rescue her successfully, you put her in my car, and I go with her."

The three looked at each other. "And if we say no?" the small man said.

"Then I blow the whole thing. I call the Blue House and warn them not to move her on Saturday. You lose your inside knowledge. She takes her chances in a trial. Do I make myself clear?"

"We could kill you right here and now," the woman said.

"Not if you are the Christians you claim to be. Conceivably Christians might kill a dictator, but not a fellow Christian. If you are part of the regime, yes you could, you probably would kill me, but not if you are Christians."

The three looked at each other, using telepathy to communicate. At last the tall man began to smile. The other two smiled back, and then they all began to laugh. "You are right," the tall man said. "You have it all figured out. All right then. We do it your way. Be ready at dawn. The move will come early in the day, before traffic gets bad. Our cars must all be near prison then."

"I'm sure I will not sleep," Boyce said.

They let him out the back door of the noodle shop and closed the metal door behind him. The alley was dark and menacing. Boyce could see cars passing on a main road to the right and made a dash that way. As he reached the corner a man touched him on the arm and spoke in broken English. "Hey man, you want woman? I give you hot girl for hour, top the line."

Boyce shook his arm free. "Get away from me," he hissed. "Leave me alone, you loathsome creature." Boyce was surprised at his contempt. He sounded like one of his Presbyterian forebears. He walked on.

The man followed him, hissing: "Mighty fine time you have, see girl naked. Korea girl."

Boyce turned and faced him. "That would not be new for me. I've just seen a Korean girl naked."

"Top the line."

"She was, she was top the line."

10

americans

O n Friday morning Boyce was looking out his window at the street and noticed a man leaning against a light post on the corner. Something jolted his memory, and he realized he had seen the man before. The man had a shock of hair that fell over his forehead and a scar across the right side of his face, from throat to ear. Boyce had suspected that he would be watched and followed, but this was the first evidence of it.

After breakfast he went out the front door and strolled down the street, stopping every block to window shop. Each time he glanced back he saw the man. He had no plans to meet the conspirators, but it galled him to know that he was under surveillance. He walked until he saw a butcher's shop with both the front and back doors open. He went in and walked straight through to the alley behind the store. He trotted up the alley to the next street and came out. The tail was nowhere to be seen. He turned into an arcade and wound his way through the stalls, coming out several streets away from where he had entered. Still no signs of the man with the hair and scar.

He jumped on a city bus and rode it as it maneuvered through the traffic and eventually left the congested part of the city and entered the nearest thing to open countryside outside Seoul. To the side of the road rose a hillside with new buildings on it. Signs announced that this was Seoul National University. He remembered S.N.U. from the days when it was a fledgling little school crammed into a crowded neighborhood in the heart of the city. In America he had read that one day as President Yi played golf on the course where the university now stood he told one of his aids: "This would be a nice place for a school." His wish was the aid's command. Ground was broken the next spring, and by fall classes had moved out from downtown to this idyllic spot in the hills.

Boyce got off the bus and made his way up a cobble stone path leading to the classroom buildings. Scattered about on benches under trees, taking in the fresh air, so different from the air in the city where they lived, sat students, mostly males, talking, laughing, carrying on various forms of high jinks. He had read, as he observed Korean from afar, that S.N.U. had become the nation's premier institution of higher learning, surpassing the schools established first by religious groups, Catholic and Protestant. Stories reported that S.N.U. accepted only the top two percent of high school graduates, that school kids studied like fiends to make high enough test scores to be admitted, and that once in they did not study, they learned the social skills they had not had time to develop while they slaved away in high school. He had heard, from Korean graduate students in the U.S., that a teacher at S.N.U. could be fired for giving too much work, that no one at S.N.U. ever made below an A in any course, and that a student could be sent to prison for ten years if he spoke out against the government.

Boyce spent the morning observing Korea's future leaders. He noted that many of the boys sat holding hands with other boys and that the few girls sat holding hands with other girls. In a few cases the couples sat cheek to cheek. He knew that until university the public schools were segregated, and he supposed that most of the students here had never been introduced to members of the opposite sex. He thought that this type of homoerotic dalliance had probably been common in Europe before coeducation became common.

At a certain time, without a bell or signal of any kind that Boyce heard or saw, more than half of the loungers got up from benches and grass and headed toward classroom buildings. Boyce strolled over and took one of the emptied benches. After a moment he noticed a young lady, sitting on a bench opposite him, intently reading a book. She apparently had no class to attend at that hour. The longer he watched her the more he saw that she looked very much like Ji-wan, the way Ji-wan looked when she was that age, the age when he had known her just before he left for America. She glanced up and saw him watching her, and he expected her to avert her eyes the way most Korean girls did when they confronted a man, especially a foreigner; but she looked at him for a long time. She seemed to be trying to remember where she had seen him. Then she smiled.

Boyce nodded and smiled back at her; but he hesitated about making any other gesture of friendship. The young girl closed the book she was reading, gathered her other books, stood, and walked away. Only when she was gone did he reflect on the encounter. He began to wonder whether she had been real. Perhaps he only imagined her. Perhaps what the mystics said was true, that she was a vision, a spiritual personification of his memory of Ji-wan. Perhaps Ji-wan was communicating with him through a vapor that only appeared to be real. Whatever the case, he knew it was time to go. He shook himself and got up.

Boyce caught the first bus into town and went back to his hotel. Across the street from the front door stood the man with the hair and scar. Boyce pretended not to see him, and the man pretended not to see Boyce.

On the bed in his room he found several newspapers, three in Korean, two in English. On the front pages of them all he saw the same picture: President Yi shaking the hand of Professor Boyce Mann, grandson of the first Presbyterian missionary to Korea, both smiling at the camera, apparently friends and allies.

Boyce did not see the man with the scar when he went out to catch a taxi to the ambassador's residence at sunset. When he arrived outside the gate of the palatial home of the American envoy, he was mildly surprised to see his brother Andrew waiting for him.

"So you are invited too," he said.

"Yes," Andrew smiled. "I guess they want all the Manns, not just the one come from a distant land. I don't get many invitations to fancy do's; so I guess I have you to thank for this one." He saluted.

"Come on," Boyce grinned. "It's not me they want, it's not even you and me together, it's our name, you know that. But I guess it's our obligation to make the best of it."

"Saw you in the papers," Andrew said. "You seem to be making the rounds to all the best people."

"Yes," Boyce said sardonically.

"Shall we?" Andrew held out an arm toward the gate.

"Why not?"

The U.S. Marine guard at the gate knew them by sight and admitted them to the grounds. He pointed toward the front porch, and they strolled among the flowers slowly, to show they were neither anxious nor reticent to arrive. Another Marine at the door admitted them immediately upon seeing who they were.

No sooner had they entered the ambassador's large, well furnished living than a waiter served them glasses of Champaign, and immediately they were confronted by Eriksen and Shu, looking like ill matched Siamese twins. They both shook hands with both brothers, Shu smiling, Eriksen frowning. "So far no repercussions," Eriksen said without bothering with small talk.

"Repercussions?" Andrew said.

"I spoke to the president a bit too forthrightly for Mr. Eriksen's taste," Boyce said. "He gave me orders, and I didn't follow them."

"I am sure you meant no harm," Shu said to Boyce. "I'm sure your brother meant no harm," he said to Andrew.

"What did you do?" Andrew said, both intrigued and slightly alarmed.

"He asked me questions, and I answered them," Boyce said.

"A little too, as you said, forthrightly," Eriksen said.

"Perhaps," Boyce admitted.

"Well, enjoy yourselves," Eriksen said. He walked away, and Shu followed him. They joined a clump of people near the fireplace.

"Nice chap," Boyce said.

"Yes, well, he has a hard job, trying to put out brush fires," Andrew said. "Plus, there's his personal life."

"What?"

"His wife's just left him, gone home, asked for a divorce."

"What happened?"

"They say she just had enough. They've been in Libya and Ghana, now here, and the pressure was too much for her. He looks more weather beaten every time I see him. So did she, every time I saw her."

A man emerged from another clump of people and came toward them. He shook Andrew's hand, and Andrew introduced him. "Boyce, this is Wright White. Wright, my brother Boyce Mann."

White's handshake was firm but cold. His light blue eyes were icy. "We're here because of you, I believe," White said.

"Maybe," Boyce said. "I wouldn't know."

"Excuse me, I need to get a refill on my drink," Andrew said and left them.

"You are with the embassy?" Boyce asked.

"Uh yes," White said. "Understand you teach at Davidson."

"That's right. I'm trying to place your accent. Definitely southern, but not deep southern."

White seemed disturbed at being placed. "I thought I had covered it up, he said tartly. Then he softened just a bit. "Originally I'm from Kentucky."

"Kentucky. What city? I've been there often for conferences."

"Different towns," White said.

"And college?"

"There too."

"What do you do with the embassy?"

"I'd rather... It's not wise to say exactly. A bit sensitive." He cleared his throat. "Understand you met the president."

"Yes, it seems to have made the papers."

"How'd it go?"

"Well, I thought, but I seem to have upset Eriksen."

"I know. You were a little too frank, he said."

"I tried to be truthful."

"Sometimes that's not good."

"I find it hard to understand why the United States looks the other way when he breaks every principle we say we hold sacred."

White's eyes narrowed. "The world is not a simple place," he said. "We have to do a lot of things we wish we didn't have to do. Before Yi took over there was chaos here. In the late 50s, if things had gone on the way they were, we would have lost this country. Communists would have taken over. With his military background—and military backing—he gave stability, which is about all we can hope for at present."

"The communist threat works well for him."

"Listen," White said. "You gotta understand, these people are children. They're like we were five hundred years ago, when we needed a king like Henry VIII to tell us what to do. They'll grow up if we give them time, but right now they can no more run a democracy than they can flap their arms and fly." He was panting slightly. "Believe me, they need Yi Dong-ho, a father, a king, to bring them to maturity."

"He is a father and a king all right," Boyce said. He remembered his lessons about Henry VIII: tight control over the whole country, destruction in his wake.

"I thank God every day for him," White said.

"I imagine so," Boyce nodded.

"Gentlemen!" a resonant bass voice interrupted their conversation, and they turned to see a large, well dressed man coming toward them, a small well dressed woman in tow.

Boyce and White turned. White smiled broadly. "Mister Ambassador," he said. "Ambassador Bernard Kaye, Mrs. Kelly-Kaye, may I introduce the guest of honor, Professor Boyce Mann."

"Professor," the ambassador said, flashing a smile that demonstrated the look and personality that had made him a multimillionaire corporate executive, a major contributor to Republican Party candidates, including Richard Nixon, and now U.S. Ambassador to South Korea. "I am most happy to meet you at last. I have read a lot about you and your family." He flashed the smile again. "Oh, and this is my wife, Mrs. Kaye, Polyanna Kelly-Kaye."

Boyce shook hands with them both. "Good to meet you too, Mr. and Mrs. Kaye," he said. "I've read a lot about you too."

"Don't you believe a word of it," Kaye joked. "Well, maybe half. Believe only the better half, which is my wife."

"I always take what I read in the media with a grain of salt," Boyce said.

"That's good," White interjected.

"There are a lot of liars out there, to be sure," Kaye said. "I never knew what outlandish drivel they could dredge up, make up actually because it's all fiction, and print without fear of being sued—not until I took his assignment. In private life I never had to deal with such nonsense."

"Nonsense is right," his wife said. "Why do you know they're even critical of me for my antique collecting. I love Korean antique furniture, and they say I'm using diplomatic transfer post to steal national treasures."

"It's ridiculous," Kaye said. "If I'd known I would be living in a fishbowl I'd never have taken the job." He flashed his smile and laughed but both smile and laugh were bitter.

"Anti-Semites!" his wife said. "That's all it is. If Ambassador Kaye were a Christian, a Baptist or even a Catholic, you wouldn't hear any of this. If he were a Democrat, you wouldn't hear any of it. It's just that the liberal newspapers can't abide a Republican Jew. They're all run by Democrat Jews. And those Jews don't like this kind of Jew. Why, they call Bernard Nixon's favorite Semite."

"Now, dear, let's not say something we might regret," Kaye said. "You are Christian enough for us both." He turned to Boyce with a smile. "There are great advantages to marrying a pretty Irish lass, but one of them is not her reticence."

"Yes," Boyce said.

"Anyhow, enough about us and our complaints, Professor Mann, tell me, how are you enjoying your visit?"

"It's been an experience," Boyce said. "Things have changed a lot since I lived here in the late 40s."

"Oh, I'm sure of that," Kaye nodded. "Lots of progress, I'm sure you'd agree. President Yi has performed a veritable miracle."

"Wonderful man," his wife said. "And that young daughter of his, what a brave soul. She has taken on an incredible task, doing the work her mother did with such passion and competence. I admire that girl so much. She is a wonder."

"Yes she is, dear," Kaye said with feeling. "Have you read about her, Professor Mann?"

"Uh, yes," Boyce said. "I even met her."

"No. She is an angel, isn't she?"

Just then a photographer appeared, and Kaye nodded to him. "Professor, how about a picture? You and the president made the newspapers, and I don't see why you and I can't." He put one large arm around his wife and the other around Boyce and turned the three of them toward the photographer. "Now all of us need to smile."

They smiled loyally as the photographer snapped over and over, and when he was finished Kaye gripped Boyce's hand. "Thank you so much for coming, Professor. I do admire what you and your family have done for Korea. You'll have to excuse me, but President Ford will be calling me in a few minutes, so I have to go. But please let my wife introduce you to all the guests, and have some of this wonderful food and drink that my doctors tell me I can't have." He laughed and abruptly left Boyce and the wife to carry on.

Boyce met the dozen or so guests, ate and drank his fill, and a bit earlier than he had expected found himself saying good night and leaving the grounds with Andrew. They walked up the street together.

"Enjoy yourself?" Andrew said.

"Some," Boyce answered.

"Boyce, I haven't seen you much... "

"Yes, I'm sorry about that... "

Andrew stopped and faced his brother. "No, it's all right. I understand. It's probably for the best. But let me give you a brotherly warning. You don't understand what's going on here. You've been away too long. I know you have seen Ji-wan, and I know various people have contacted you. Be extremely careful. You can never know who you're talking to in this environment. You could get yourself into deep trouble. Myself, I stay completely out of it all."

"I know, Andrew, and I appreciate that. You have your life to live, and that life is here. Mine is not. I won't do anything to jeopardize your security or safety. I know I'm naïve. I also know that I love Ji-wan."

"Stay out of it, Boyce," Andrew said with feeling. "It's not our war."

"It's our birthright."

"What does that mean?"

"We are Manns, whether we like it or not. The Manns and Korea are one."

"Not this Mann. I live here, I'll always live here, but I have no obligation to save anyone but myself. I certainly have no obligation to save Korea."

"Our parents did. Our grandparents did."

"Not me. Not you either. You much less even than me. Please, Boyce, you should leave well enough alone."

Boyce smiled. "Andrew, there is a new association in America, one organized so that Christians of all denominations and Jews of all branches can have dialogue. Their motto is: We agree to disagree agreeably. I guess that's what you and I can do. Right?"

Andrew stated at him. "Boyce, I don't understand you." He shrugged. "But then I never understood mom and dad either."

11

escape

B oyce was fully awake at 4:00 a.m. the next morning. He tried to remain in bed, hoping to go back to sleep, but at last he uttered a mild curse and got up. After a shower he stood at his window and watched the city awaken. It was Saturday, but the men working on the building across the street were already busy. He watched as beggars emerged from their alleys and took up their customary places in front of the stores, preparing for a day of playing on the sympathies of passersby. He remembered how store keepers in Florence warned beggars away from their sidewalks because they felt the beggars frightened away customers. He realized he never saw beggars in Charlotte.

As he returned from his breakfast he told the desk clerk that he was expecting a car to come for him. He explained, in far more detail than the clerk would have needed to know if the story were true, how he planned to go out into the countryside to visit several farmers who had known his parents. He said he might or might not be back for the night. The clerk took notes on what he said, even though he looked doubtful that the information would ever be relevant.

He returned to his room and waited. Time passed slowly. He wondered whether the conspirators would back out on their plan, whether they would simply leave him out of the picture, knowing he would have no leverage against them after the fact. He walked the floor and pounded softly on doors. He ran to the telephone when it rang at 10:00.

"Yes?" he said hoarsely.

"Your car is waiting, sir," the clerk said.

Boyce walked as quickly as he could down the hallway and the stairs without appearing to be in a hurry. In the lobby stood the short man, wearing a suit what appeared to be a chauffer's uniform.

"Doctor Mann?" the man asked.

"Yes, that right. You will drive me to Tau-san?"

"Yes sir."

The short man led him out to a car that resembled one of the multitude of taxis in the street, common enough not to draw attention and not to be identified later on. Boyce got in, and they pulled away. As they left he spotted the man with the scar standing on the sidewalk. The man looked away up the street as they passed him.

"Why are you so late?" Boyce asked.

"The transfer will be later than we thought," the driver said.

"How do you know?"

"We have... informants."

"Other than me."

"Yes."

After taking a circuitous route through town, which was not as busy as on week day mornings, the driver pulled up across the street and a block away from the prison gate through which Boyce had passed on his way to see Ji-wan. The driver got out and pulled the decals that indicated this was a rented car and driver off the sides of the car and put them on the floorboard beside him.

"What now?" Boyce said.

"We wait. Look up ahead. Three cars along the street beyond the gate? Those are ours."

"I see."

"We all wait."

Wait they did. Boyce watched the dash board clock as the minutes slowly ticked off. Noon came and went. Boyce felt slightly hungry, and he needed a pee break, but he knew they had to stay put.

It was nearing 2:00 when the driver stirred. Something Boyce had not seen had caught his attention. He started his engine. After a long moment the two guards inside the prison gate pushed the gate open and emerged to stand to either side of it. Boyce and the driver watched as a single van came through the gate and turned right onto the street. The van was dark green, without any markings, which meant the prison officials wanted to be as inconspicuous as possible. It made its way slowly down the street. The three cars Boyce's driver had pointed out eased out and followed it. Boyce's driver followed them.

Nothing happened until the van came to the center of town, where traffic picked up, and then one of the cars passed the van, another drove up beside it, and the third moved directly behind it. Boyce's driver remained behind them all. Then the car ahead of the van stopped suddenly, making the van's driver throw on his brakes, the car behind it pulled in so close that it could not back up, and the car beside it stopped to block any escape.

Men piled out of all three cars and with bats smashed out the van's front windows. They reached in and opened both doors and roughly pulled the driver and his companion out onto the street. They wrestled them to the ground, took their pistols, and threw them as far away as they could send them. A man sat on each one as the others rushed around and forced open the van's back doors. Shots rang out as guards inside the van defended themselves, and two of the abductors fell to the pavement; but these two guards were also outnumbered, and they were pulled out, forced to the ground, and disarmed like the other two.

Two abductors jumped into the back of the van and after a moment came out with the tiny woman they were sent to rescue. Ji-wan looked dazed and frightened, but the men did not take time to explain to her what they were doing. They rushed her to the lead car, her legs wobbling, and the other abductors ran for the other two cars, leaving the two who were wounded or maybe dead in the street beside the four stunned guards. Boyce's driver fell into a convoy behind the other three cars.

Two policemen on motorcycles had either spotted the abduction or were alerted to it; and they came rushing down the street toward the cars with sirens blaring. They passed the car carrying Boyce and Ji-wan and gave chase behind the other three for several blocks before one of them hit an abutment and went flying into the air from an overpass that he took too fast and the other plowed into a crowd of pedestrians crossing at a light. The first was probably dead, the second put out of commission. Boyce's driver laughed loudly as each cop ended his pursuit. Boyce thought it was not a Christian response to tragedy but then realized there was little Christian about this whole scene.

When the convoy reached the outskirts of the city, the lead car pulled over, and the others stopped behind it. Boyce's driver pulled up alongside the lead car, and the four men in it brought Ji-wan out and over to him. Boyce opened his door, and she slowly got in and sat beside him. She looked at him and seemed to recognize him because she smiled vaguely, but she was in shock and quickly laid her head back against the seat and closed her eyes. Boyce's car drove off straight ahead, and the other three followed for a time before they peeled off and went in three separate directions.

Boyce put his arm around Ji-wan and encouraged her to lie down on the seat with her head on his lap. As far as he knew, his car had not been identified as part of the abduction, but he didn't want to run the risk that someone would spot Ji-wan and report where she was. He stroked her hair softly and hummed a tune quietly as they drove. He saw welts on her neck and arms, proof that she had been beaten. They made his blood boil.

He was so intent on comforting Ji-wan that he paid no attention to where they were going. It was an hour before rough roads caused him to look out the window. Right away he spotted a hillside that looked familiar to him. It took him a time to calibrate it, but after a time he realized that they were headed toward the old family retreat. They were bouncing along a dirt road, unchanged, unimproved since the turn of the century.

"We are going to Be-san?" he asked the driver.

"Yes. It is safe place."

"The government doesn't know about my family's retreat there?"

"No one been there since your father died there in 1953. No member of family, no one from church."

"Is the cabin still standing?"

"We see."

The sun was beginning its downward plunge when the driver pulled off the dirt road and started up what appeared to be a cow trail. They passed a peasant house, where an elderly couple stood up from hoeing in a garden to stare at them. The man raised a hand in salute. Up and up the hillside they wound until they came to the clearing Boyce remembered so vividly. The family retreat house still stood, weather beaten, slightly askew, slanted to one side but recognizable. Three men and two women appeared at the front door and came out to help them bring Ji-wan across the rough yard and inside the house.

There was little furniture, none Boyce recognized from the time he had spent summer holidays here, only a table and chairs, a ragged sofa, and a bed. The women talked with Ji-wan, asking her if she could eat, and she said no, asking her if she wanted to sleep, and she said yes. So the women helped her lie down and covered her with a quilt. One of the women took a chair beside her bed and the other signaled for the men, including Boyce, to leave them and come out to the front porch.

The woman went to the trunk of the getaway car and brought them bread and fruit and jugs of water. As the sun set they ate and wondered what was going on down in the city. Part of the plot was to keep silence, not to communicate with the outside world, to avoid being overheard and detected and found. Finally, exhausted, each of the men found a place on the porch to curl up and sleep, while the woman went inside to stay with Ji-wan and the second woman.

At the first light of morning Boyce got up from his hard wooden bed and went out into the yard. He remembered where his mother had cultivated her beloved roses and saw that the only reminder of them was a patch of briars. His father's lilies were gone to crabgrass. The beautiful world he had known as a boy had died with his parents, and all that was left were ugly imitations of the goodness they had hoped to plant. Their church was now divided into sycophants and rebels, the first living in harmony with evil, the second volunteering to be hunted animals. He was not sure how he would leave this place—or whether he ever would leave it alive.

The men on the porch were snoring, and there was no sign of life from inside the cabin. Boyce let him mind stray out beyond the property his parents owned to the hills behind it. He remembered that as boys he and Andrew had often climbed up to the top of the mountain and there stopped to listen to the chanting of the Buddhist monks in their abbey. He wondered if they were still there. Since he felt he was not needed at the cabin, he decided to have a look.

It was hard to remember the exact path he and his brother had taken. Many of the trails had eroded away; others were covered with bushes. It took him over an hour to make what had once been a twenty minute trek; but at last, panting for breath, he came to the old clearing near the top of the mountain and saw the familiar buildings, covered with the odd reverse swastika symbol of Buddhism. As his breath returned to normal he could hear chanting, and he went forward as in the old days and listened.

The words were medieval Korean, a mixture of the native language and Chinese and even a few Indian words, demonstrating the pathway the religion had taken from its origin through its movement across the continent to this remote peninsula. The voices were clear and on key, and Boyce recalled that the monastery had always chosen the best ears and voices from among their members to do their singing. One voice, at times solo hovering above a communal humming, was as pure as any Boyce had ever heard in professional opera. The monk could have been a rich man had he chosen to stay in the world and pursue fame.

While he was listening a young woman, no more than fifteen, came out of the main building and stood on the front porch smiling at him. He nodded to her, and she came down the steps to him.

"You are welcome, pilgrim," she said in Korean.

"Thank you," he responded.

"You are a white man, yet you speak our language."

"I was born here."

"Here? On this holy mountain?"

"In Seoul."

"I am Su," she said.

"Boyce."

"Boyce, why are you here, in this holy place?"

"I... " Boyce was not sure what to say, he was not sure why he was here. "I come... for enlightenment." He knew this was the goal of Buddhists because he had known so many of them during his boyhood.

"That is good," the girl said. "That is why I am here." She took his hand and led him to a bench under a tree and had him sit beside her. "I have felt the hand of God on my shoulder, heard the voice of God in the night, know that I am called to give up the world and spend my life in prayer and meditation."

Boyce had heard of girls like this, girls who felt they had a divine calling to be Shamans, girls who turned their backs on the world to serve monks.

"My father hates me," she said, and tears came to her eyes. "He thinks I am throwing my life away. He does not know I am actually following the divine pathway to eternal life. He has disowned me. I could not return home now even if I wanted to do so. I am God's orphan." She looked into Boyce's eyes. "Are you a believer?"

"A believer? Well, I'm not sure."

"Buddha loves you and will give you assurance."

"I am... my family is... Christian."

"That's all right," the girl said. "You can be a Christian and follow Lord Buddha. Your Jesus is a manifestation of Buddha, perhaps the most perfect manifestation. You can find enlightenment by following Jesus to the Lord Buddha who gives truth to us all."

She came near Boyce and leaned her head on his shoulder. "Just give yourself to Him, and he will give you the peace you do not now have."

They sat together like that for a long time. At last the chanting ceased and the girl stirred, pulled away, and stood. "I must go now, to serve the monks," she said, smiling down at Boyce. "But you stay here, pray, ask for enlightenment, and it will come, I promise." Then she was gone, back up the steps, into the building.

Boyce sat on the bench for a long time, thinking that what the girl had said was doubtless true, that it might be a formula for a peaceful Korea.

Then his reverie was shattered by gunfire. Three shots, then four more. He jumped to his feet and looked down the mountain; but he couldn't see the cabin. More gunfire. He started back down, trying to remember how he had come, stumbling, falling several times. Halfway through the journey he saw smoke and then flames, and he knew the cabin was burning.

As he broke through the last of the scrub bushes, Boyce saw a green van driving away from the burning building. The car that brought him and Ji-wan was also burning. Scattered around the yard were bodies. He ran from one to the other and found all four of the men, including his driver, and one of the women dead. As he stood amid the carnage in shock, he heard sobbing and looked to see the other woman coming out of the trees to the side of the cabin. He ran to her, and she fell into his arms.

"No, no, no!" she wailed.

"What happened?" he said, trying to calm her.

"They came, they shot, they killed, they burned!" she cried out.

"Where... where is Ji-wan?"

"She... they... gone!"

"Gone? They took her?"

"Yes!"

He loosened her grip and pushed her away from him, holding her arms. "Be quiet," he hissed. "Stop crying. You must get control of yourself."

She continued to wail. Boyce raised his hand and gave her a soft slap across her cheek. She wailed on. He slapped her harder. Her eyes focused and she looked at him and began fighting him, using both fists to strike him in the chest. He drew back and slapped her as hard as he could. She fell to the ground and embraced his legs and wept bitterly. He sat down beside her, took her in his arms, and they cried together until they were both exhausted.

At long last he asked the woman if she could stand, and she nodded. They got up. "We must put these people in a place together where you can watch over them," he told her. She nodded again. The flames of the cabin and the car had burned down to smoke, and the two of them drug the bodies to a protected spot in the trees.

"You must stay here, keep watch over our people, and I will send help. Are you able to do that?" he asked the woman. She nodded.

Reluctantly Boyce left the yard and followed the rutted road down to the peasant's house. The man stood outside and said nothing to Boyce as he approached him.

"Did you see what happened?" Boyce asked.

The man shook his head.

"Good. Tell anyone who asks that you saw nothing. But get word to the police. Have them investigate the fire. They will take care of everything. Can you do that, Father?"

The man nodded.

Boyce saw a bicycle leaning against the rail fence that surrounded the man's yard. "Is that yours?"

The man nodded.

Boyce reached into his coat pocket and pulled out several bills, more than enough to pay for the old, dented vehicle. He handed them to the man. "I need to take it. You may never see it again, but that will buy you a new one. Is that all right with you, Father?"

The man nodded.

Boyce took the bike and jumped on it. It was decrepit but useable. He had not ridden a bike for many years; but he found he could balance well enough. The road was rough, but he maneuvered around the largest holes and within an hour found himself on a paved highway. Signs directed him toward Seoul. It was well past noon before he came to the edge of the city, where he left the bike behind a wall and hailed a cab. In another hour, because of light Sunday traffic, he got out at his hotel.

Three policemen were waiting for him in the lobby. They called him by his full name and showed him their badges.

"Where have you been, Professor Mann?" one of them said.

"In the country," Boyce said, trying to sound confident. "You can tell by all my dust and sweat."

"Doing what in the country?"

"Visiting old friends. Friends of my parents. The clerk can verify that."

The policemen looked at the desk clerk, the same one Boyce had carefully told his story the day before, and the clerk confirmed that Boyce had left with a driver, saying he was going to visit friends.

"Who are those friends?" one of the policemen said. "Names, please, and their addresses."

Boyce made up names and addresses, hoping the cops wouldn't check them out, playing the odds that they were too busy with other matters to do so.

"You had a car and driver?"

"Yes."

"But you returned in a taxi. Why is that?"

"I had the bad luck to be given a driver who drinks," Boyce said, knowing the Korean weakness for alcohol. "His driving frightened me. As soon as we came to the city and the traffic picked up, I dismissed him and took a taxi the rest of the way."

The cops looked at Boyce for a long moment and then broke into laughter. They understood drunken drivers.

"We found your room open," one of them said. "The door was ajar."

"Guess I'm that absent minded professor you hear about," Boyce said. He wondered whether he had left the door open or someone had searched his room, someone not with the police; but he left it with a joke at his own expense.

The cops laughed again.

"I guess that will be all," the leader said. They started to go. "Oh yes," he turned back, "I have a message from the government. A car will pick you up at 8:00 tomorrow morning to take you to the court... to observe a trial, I believe."

Boyce tried to hide his surprise. The authorities obviously suspected him of being a part of the abduction. Why else would they question him about his recent meanderings? Why then was he still permitted, more than permitted actually summoned to attend the trial? At least the trial, still scheduled for Monday, meant that Ji-wan was not dead, perhaps not even badly wounded by the attack on the cabin. Boyce went to his room, his head spinning, fell across his bed, and went immediately to sleep.

12

verdict

When he woke at daybreak, Boyce was ravenous. He realized he had not eaten a substantial meal for two days. But before he went down to breakfast he went to the vending machine at the end of his hallway and bought a newspaper. The headlines were about a melee at the Demilitarized Zone. The limbs of a tree in No Man's Land were blocking the view of South Korean soldiers keeping an eye on North Korean installations; and a crew of four Americans went out with axes to cut them off. Ten North Korean soldiers appeared, took the axes away from the Americans, and attacked them with the weapons. Two Americans were badly cut. An official inquiry was being conducted. A meeting between high representatives of both sides was scheduled.

Boyce searched from front to back of the small paper but found no mention of Kim Ji-wan, nothing about the trial, nothing about the abduction. He was not sure whether this was a good sign or a bad one. Still puzzling over it all, he went down to breakfast, and despite having a nervous stomach he ate the heartiest meal since his arrival in Seoul.

At exactly 8:00 a.m. a Korean soldier entered the hotel lobby, bowed to him, and escorted him out to a waiting government car. The soldier let Boyce get into the back seat and himself took a seat beside the driver. They eased through the morning traffic and at last came to a building that showed no outward evidence of being a government structure, let alone a court house. On the sidewalk out front, waiting for him, stood Eriksen.

"You came," he said.

"Yes," Boyce said with a shrug. "It's a command performance, or should I say command appearance."

Eriksen either did not catch or chose not to respond to the attempt at humor. He took Boyce's arm and led him away from the car. "Now this time," he said, "you listen to me, and you do exactly what I tell you to do."

"It appears I have little choice," Boyce said, pulling his arm free of Eriksen's grasp with enough force to free it but gently enough not to attract attention.

"Not if you want to get out of this alive."

"That serious, is it?"

"We know all about it."

"About what?"

"Don't be a smart ass. You're too conspicuous to get away with it and not be seen. They know too."

"Yet I'm free, I'm even a guest at the trial."

"They have their reasons," Eriksen hissed. "Believe me, they have their reasons. You're living on borrowed time."

"Guess I'd better make the most of it then."

Eriksen snorted. "Listen, though, in there, you keep your mouth shut. I mean don't say a word. Just smile and nod and do as you're told."

"I had planned to do just that."

"Yeah, well you have a way of throwing monkey wrenches into the works. Don't do it in there."

"Gotcha, boss."

"It's not funny."

"I know."

Eriksen took his arm again and led him to the door. A guard admitted them, and Eriksen took Boyce down a long hallway and knocked on a door. Another guard opened and admitted them into a large room, apparently adapted from a typing pool into a court. There were twenty or so chairs for spectators to view proceedings, a raised desk for a judge, two smaller desks facing him, apparently for lawyers, and a chair for witnesses. Half a dozen spectators sat on the right side of the room, and Eriksen and Boyce sat as far from them as possible on the left.

After what seemed to Boyce like an eternity, a side door opened, and the judge entered and took his seat at the high table. The two lawyers followed him and sat at the two tables. Some time later a guard brought Ji-wan in and had her sit in the witness box. She looked exhausted and dazed. Boyce wondered if she had been kept awake through the night, if she had been abused again, if she were drugged. One of the lawyers stood.

"Sir, I have questions for the defendant." Korean has several levels of formality in the language, and this man used the highest. The judge represented the person of the king.

"Just a moment," the judge said in a form used to address servants. He turned to Ji-wan. "Do you understand that you are accused of complicity in the attempt to assassinate the President of the Republic of Korea, Yi Dong-ho?" he asked her.

Ji-wan sat with her head down and her eyes on the floor. She gave no sign that she heard the question.

"Do you understand?" the judge insisted.

Still no response.

"Very well," the judge said, "since I have made it clear to you the charges you face, I shall assume you understand." He looked at the lawyer. "Proceed."

The lawyer went forward and stood before Ji-wan. She did not lift her eyes. "Kim Ji-wan," he said, "I have three questions for you. In order to avoid punishment for the crime you are accused of committing, you must answer all three of these questions." He waited for a response. "Do you understand?"

For the first time Ji-wan raised her eyes, looked directly into the lawyer's eyes, and nodded.

"Good," he said. "Yesterday an attempt was made to abduct you, to take you out of the hands of justice. Who planned that plot?"

Ji-wan continued to look into the lawyer's eyes, but she made no reply.

"Name the persons involved."

No reply.

"Were communists involved? Were foreigners?"

Nothing.

The lawyer sighed. "Well then, the second question. You have publicly defended those arrested for the attempted assassination of our President, those who indeed succeeded in killing our First Lady. Why did you do such a thing?"

Ji-wan took a breath and seemed about to speak, but then she closed her lips and remained silent.

"Were you trying to help friends, fellow Christians, or do you sympathize with their plans to lop off the head of our government?"

A smile played about Ji-wan's lips, but she said nothing.

"Well then, my third and final question. I must warn you that your silence, your refusal to answer these questions, will be judged an admission of guilt. The question is, were you involved in the planning of the assassination attempt on our President which ended with the death of our First Lady?"

The lawyer was prepared for more silence, and he was surprised when Ji-wan at last spoke. Her voice was low but firm, soft but strong.

"My answer is yes, I knew about the plot, I gave the conspirators my approval, indeed my blessing, and I prayed to God that they would succeed. I deeply regret the death of the First Lady, a woman I greatly admired, but I believed and still believe that the death of the President would be a blessing to our nation. I believed it was my Christian duty to aid those who planned to end his tyrannical rule over us."

There was complete silence in the court room. Boyce felt sick. The lawyer, looking shocked, bowed to the judge and took his seat. The judge looked toward the other lawyer, but that man shook his head and remained seated. The judge cleared his throat and looked at Ji-wan.

"Do you make this confession of your own free will, without undue pressure being placed on you? Is what you have said the truth?"

Ji-wan nodded. "Yes."

The judge sighed. "Then I have no alternative than to have you committed to prison for a period of one month, long enough for you to settle all of your accounts, and then for you to be shot."

Boyce saw and heard the rest of the proceedings as if in an echo chamber surrounded by wavering mirrors. Ji-wan disappeared, then the judge, then the lawyers, then the spectators; and then he felt Eriksen tugging at his arm. "Let's go," he was saying.

Then they were outside, on the sidewalk, and Boyce was losing his breakfast in the gutter, with Eriksen keeping him on his feet and pleading with him to get control of himself. Then he was walking, alone, down the street, and Eriksen was gone.

Boyce didn't know how long he walked, he didn't really know where he was, he wanted to be lost in the big city. Ji-wan was going to die. He didn't care whether he lived or not.

Without warning four men broke into his world. Walking on four sides of him, they wordlessly guided him into an alley and through a door into the back room of what smelled like a fish market. A dim light bulb gave off a loud buzz. Once more Boyce wanted to throw up, but fear kept him continent.

"We are Ji-wan's people," one of the men said. Boyce looked at him. He was the man with the shock of hair and the scar on his face, the one who had been watching him from the street corner outside the hotel, the one who had tried and failed to tail him.

"You?" Boyce said. "You're with Ji-wan?"

"He is," an American voice cut through the dim light's buzz. Boyce saw that it was Wright White, the Kentuckian, the one Boyce assumed was CIA. "I vouch for all of them."

"You? What... " Boyce was trying to make sense of what was happening to him. "I don't... "

"Just listen," White said. "We have to act quickly. Hundreds of lives hang in the balance. Not just Ji-wan's, hundreds of others.

Those who were involved in the assassination plot. Those involved in the plot to help her escape. Ji-wan was not involved in either plot. She knew nothing about the assassination. She lied this morning to save them. She thought she could carry the cross for them, all; but she was, she is terribly naïve. The truth is about to come out, and there will be a massive roundup of people, they will all die, and we must head that off."

"How will you do that?" Boyce said wearily. For the first time since he came back to Korea, it all seemed hopeless to him.

"The old man must die," White said.

"Old man?"

"Yi. He has served his purpose. It's time for him to go."

"You're going to kill Yi? You?" Boyce shook his head. "Who are you?"

White smiled. "I'm an American. I'm a friend of the Korean people."

"Come on," Boyce said.

"Believe it or not, it's true. That's all you need to know about me. Now I'm going to tell you the plan, because you are an integral part of it. You already know enough that if you do not play the hand I'm dealing you we will have to kill you as well." He let the words sink in.

"I'm integral?" Boyce said. "How?"

"Yi doesn't suspect you, not even after that stupid trick you played, going with the abductors. You should have let them do it without you, keep yourself clean. You were lucky, very lucky not to have been killed, not to have been seen."

"Oh yes."

"No sarcasm," White said. "Yi trusts you, we have made sure he does, but even more importantly you have access to his daughter."

"I do?"

"We know all about it... Father Mann."

"That... was... personal."

"Nothing is personal here. You are the favored one, the one who can see her, the one who can find out what we need to know."

"What is it you need to know?"

"On Wednesday Yi will plant a tree, a bit of symbolic nonsense, to show he supports the Arbor Movement, part of his grand plan to make Korea a modern paradise, to cover up the fact that his industrialization projects are killing the place. He will go to a remote spot, away from the crowds, away from most of his bodyguard, but with his photographer to make publicity propaganda, and while he is in the wilderness we will gun him down."

Boyce wanted to laugh, it was so melodramatic, something he might read in a novel or see in a movie but never find in real life. He knew the CIA helped plan assassinations, but he never thought he would see it happen. But why would the CIA step in now, to save these "hundreds" who might die? Maybe the hundreds were Wright White's people as much as Ji-wan's. "And my part?" he said, trying to keep a straight face.

"You get to the daughter, Father Mann, and you find out where the planting will occur. She will know, she always goes to those things. You find out, you tell us, and we will be there."

"You'll never get close to him."

"One of our people will."

"Who?"

"He doesn't know that his photographer, the one who shot you when you paid your courtesy call, has an identical twin brother, a man who works for us. The real photographer will be given a long lasting sedative and will not go on the trip, his brother will; and the camera will be in reality a gun. The old man will smile for the birdie and will be shot dead. Our other men, stationed at strategic locations with long range rifles, will shoot down his guards; and there will be no witnesses to say what happened."

Boyce shook his head.

"You find out where. That's all you do. Then you take Ji-wan out of the country on one of our planes, and you live out your life with her."

Boyce continued to shake his head.

"Remember, find out where he is going. Then get out of the way. If you don't, if you screw up, if Yi doesn't kill you, we will."

"One question," Boyce said, shaking off the threat. "Do you have the ambassador's go ahead on this plan?"

"He knows what he needs to know."

"And the President... the President of the United States?"

"Ditto."

13

the plan

Out of deference to the moral principles of his parents and grandparents, Boyce had always avoided drinking wine as a boy. In America his consumption of alcohol was merely social and never to excess. He had not had anything stronger than barley water since he returned to Korea ten days before. But that night he had rice wine with his meal, more than one glass, and with its help he was able to overcome the anxieties his meeting with White had brought him and slept soundly. The next morning he placed a call to the Blue House, the only government number he had, told the woman who answered who he was, and asked to be connected with Miss Yi. She told him she would pass his message to the proper office. Just half an hour later his phone rang.

"This is Boyce Mann," he said.

"Hello. How are you? So glad you called."

It was the First Lady. She spoke in a low, deep, seductive voice. Boyce found it both attractive and repellant.

"I'm well," he said. "And you?" He used the formal address, although she used the familiar. He was still not sure of his standing with her.

She answered familiarly, "I am tired. I need some sleep. I have been away on official business. Did you try to reach me earlier?"

"No, this is the first time."

"Can you come?"

The phrase did not have the same meaning in Korean that it did in English, but Boyce knew Miss Yi knew English, and he guessed she was aiming at a *double entendre.*

"To your residence?"

"No. I have an... unofficial residence. I will tell my driver to collect you at 10:00 and bring you here." The Korean word for "bring" did definitely have a suggestive connotation. Mistresses to the king were in old days brought to him.

"All right."

"You will not be my Father this time. You will be my little boy." She hung up before Boyce could answer.

Promptly at 10:00 a black limousine pulled up at the front of the hotel, and a chauffer jumped out to open the back door for Boyce. Boyce looked around but did not see the man with the scar. Without a word the driver closed him in, got behind the wheel, and took him to a house on a dead end street which, unusual for Seoul, was lined with trees. When he stopped, he went to the back door and let Boyce slide out onto the well kept sidewalk. Beyond a wall at the end of the street was a small copse of trees. The air here would be sweeter than in most of the city. The driver simply pointed to a house, the last one on the block, next to the wall. Boyce went up the walk and rang the bell. There was a long silence before the door opened, slowly, silently. He saw no one behind the door, and he went with some caution through it and let it close behind him. Inside an alcove, he looked down a walkway, past a stairs, and saw near the first step Miss Yi dressed in a dark gown which resembled a nun's habit.

"My little orphan boy, my little waif," she said. "Have you in all your sweet innocence come once more to help Mother Superior prepare for her rest? Well, tell me, have you?"

When Boyce did not reply because he had no idea what to say, she went on, "Come then, come with me." She started up the staircase. Not knowing what else to do, Boyce followed her.

She led him to the second floor, down another hallway, and into a room painted a muted gold. It had a narrow bed and a small desk and chair, and above the desk was an elaborate gold crucifix. The only other piece of furniture was a large easy chair with thick cushions, the only piece in the room that looked comfortable. It was as though everything else was designed to emphasize the poverty of the religious vocation, yet the chair appeared designed to satisfy the needs of a queen. Framed pictures of various saints hung at graceful intervals on the other walls. She indicated that he should close the door. He had not seen anyone else in the house, but he assumed there must be servants waiting to be summoned and that she wanted privacy, to close them out.

Once the door was closed, she looked into his eyes and then gracefully turned her back. "Now, dear boy, you must as before help Mother remove her heavy garments." She waited. "Come forward. Don't be afraid. You have done this for me many times. You know how."

Boyce felt sick, but he knew he had to play her game in order to accomplish his goal and find out where the Arbor Day event would take place. He stepped forward and came up behind her.

"Slip the cords," she said. He saw that the gown was tied in the back with a sash, and he loosened it. "Now give me freedom."

He pulled the gown, she moved forward, and it came away in his hands. She was naked. She turned to him. In their first encounter she had shown him little of her body, slipping out of the leisure suit and into his lap quickly, as if modest. This time, acting as a Mother Superior, she revealed all of her torso. Like most Asian women, she had small but firm breasts and a minimum of pubic hair. She stretched and luxuriated in her complete revelation. "You are so innocent, my little orphan, my servant boy, you are a child without sin, and what you do for Mother is perfectly all right with our God. He understands that you are the only one who can make me relax so I can sleep and regain my strength for the holy tasks I must perform. You are my sweet, innocent, pure little boy." She came to him. "Massage my breasts, little boy." She held them toward him. "It will not be a sin if a boy as innocent as you does it for me."

Boyce dropped the gown and began rubbing her breasts, first with caution and then as she gave him encouragement with more strength. She looked up at the ceiling and sighed. "Thank you, dear God, thank you," she said breathlessly. "Thank you for giving me release."

As he massaged her breasts, she opened his coat and then unbuttoned and pushed back his shirt. She came close and rubbed her breasts against his chest. "My little boy, my innocent child," she said over and over. Boyce stood stock still, letting her have her way with him, and in the process he began to feel like a child, a boy under the control of a woman he knew no better than to think holy. He felt like crying, but he held his emotions taut.

At last she sighed again and turned away, leaving him helpless, waiting for further instruction. She went over and sat down on the chair and beckoned him to come to her. When he got close enough, she quickly reached out and loosened his trousers and slipped them down, then his shorts. She looked at his tumescence. "You are so beautiful, you are so innocent, you are so pure," she said. "You are my little servant boy. You must do as I say because it is the will of God. If it is God's will, it is not wrong."

She leaned forward and took him in her mouth and began massaging him with her tongue. He fought his urges, but he felt himself losing control, and soon he felt himself gushing forth. She sighed and swallowed loudly and continued to suck him long after she had taken all he had to give her.

"So good, so very good," she said. You give me the nectar that makes me strong. You are God's little gift to me."

She lay back and opened her legs. "Now you me," she said. "It is not wrong, I am in such distress, you are pure and innocent, and I have tasted your nectar, now you must taste mine."

She pulled him toward her, and urged him to kneel. She guided his head downward and stroked his hair as he kissed and licked her. "Yes, that is good, that is good, my little boy," she said over and over until with a mighty groan she fell back and away from him and lay writhing against the cushions.

Boyce, feeling empty, feeling humiliated, waited. At last she reached out and drew him toward her and had him lie beside her on the chair. "My precious little innocent boy," she said. "It is not wrong. It is God's will."

Later she walked him down the stairs and to the front door. She seemed reluctant to see him leave, but she explained that she had duties to perform. He wanted nothing more than to be far away from her, from her smiling face, from her taunting voice, from her odor, but he knew also that he had a mission to perform and that he had not yet performed it. He tried to think how to do it. To his surprise she did it for him.

"When may I see you again?" she asked. Her voice was sad, but he knew that this could be an act like the others.

"Tomorrow?" he said. She was the last thing he wanted to see tomorrow, but he knew that tomorrow was the chosen date for the action, and he knew she could not see him then but that she might tell him where she was going with her father. It was a gamble, but it paid off.

She brightened. "Yes, tomorrow. I have something to do that you will love doing with me."

"You do? I would?" Boyce tried to sound nonchalant.

"I am going with my father to help him plant a tree."

"A tree?" Boyce tried to sound surprised, puzzled.

"He does this each year. He has his photograph made, as an example to the nation, that they should plant trees. He always took my mother with him, she was always in the picture, and this year he wants me to go and be in it with him."

"Will he mind if I go?"

"No, he likes you. He might even have you in the picture, to show his solidarity with the Americans and with our heritage. You represent both." So Boyce was now Professor Mann, not a priest, not an orphan boy. She was not delusional, she just liked to play sex games.

Boyce grimaced at the thought of being next to Yi when the photographer fired his shots, but he did not know how to refuse the invitation. He still had to find out where the ceremony would be, and he had no idea how to ask. Again to his surprise she did it for him.

"It is a beautiful place. Have you ever been to Kwok-san?"

"No. I've heard of it, but I've never been."

"It's lovely, a perfect place for the planting. It will be at a village called Wee-ban. Very small. Isolated. Safe and secure. My father must take precautions against violence." She looked deeply into his eyes. "Wee-ban," she said with emphasis. "Say it."

"Wee-ban," he repeated.

"Be ready at 9:00."

"Yes, Mother Superior."

She laughed, and her perfect white teeth flashed in the somber light of the hallway. She opened the door and let him go out. The door shut softly.

He found himself on the street, getting back into the limousine, riding away toward the city center and his hotel, replaying the scene in his mind. He had done his duty, he had found what he needed to know, what he needed to give Wright White. He had humiliated himself, offered himself like a piece of meat, to get the information; yet he had really not gained it on his own, she had given it to him without being asked.

The driver stopped, jumped out, and opened his door for him, then without a word got back into the limousine and drove away. Boyce walked to his room in a fog of confusion. He couldn't stop thinking about how she readily she had invited him on the outing, how quickly she had volunteered the name of the mountain and even the village where her father would plant his tree. In the week since he had been back in Korea he had grown suspicious. He wondered whether she knew what was being planned, whether she was a conspirator. No, surely not against her own father, he told himself, but why not? She might have reasons of her own to betray him. She might believe the stories that he had planned the assassination of his wife, her mother. In the fantasy world she inhabited, she had other fathers. She might sacrifice one for the other.

Boyce found a newspaper on his bed, and when he opened it there was a note with only two jottings: a time and a place. He knew it was the time and place for him to meet Wright White.

At 4:30, the time on the note, he stood at the place on the note, looking into a store window on a side street in the market area that served the American army base. The proprietor displayed mannequins wearing every kind of clothing from military uniforms to leisure wear to formal dress. Wright White passed behind him and without stopping whispered, "Go on inside." Boyce entered the shop. The owner smiled and bowed and without asking him what he wanted showed him a door marked in English "Fits." Boyce went through it and found White waiting for him.

"What did you find out?" White said without a word of welcome.

"What you wanted," Boyce said.

"And... "

"Before I tell you, you should know that I have to go along."

"You? Go along? To the planting? Like you went on the abduction? Oh no. We can't take you on a mission like that. It's too dangerous."

"You don't have to take me. He will. She will."

"Who?"

"The president. His daughter."

"You're joking."

"No sir. She invited me. She invited me before she told me where we were going. Then she gave me all the information I wanted, the information you wanted. She's not in on this, is she?"

"What?" White snorted. "His daughter? Don't be a fool."

"It just seemed odd how readily she gave me what should be top secret information, as if she wanted me to know more than I asked."

"That's crazy. If she were in on it, she would have told us directly. We wouldn't have needed to send you up there to play games with her."

Boyce stared at him. "Games?"

"Come off it," White grinned. "We know. But she's not with us."

"All right," Boyce said, "so she doesn't know, she just likes me, she trusts me. So if I don't go, she will get suspicious. I have to be there. I have to do what she tells me. She wants me in the pictures."

"But you can't. You might get killed."

Boyce laughed. "Korea has killed a lot of us Manns. It seems to be our mission in life."

"Damn!" White cursed.

"That's the deal. I go or the whole thing probably goes off the rails."

White sighed. He looked ready to boil over. "All right," he said with disgust. I guess that's the way it has to be. But don't you screw up."

"That's what Eriksen keeps telling me."

"Eriksen's an idiot, he's the biggest screw up of all, but I see why he would say that to you. You have no idea what this is all about, and you could mess it up without meaning to. This is the biggest thing that's gone down in this part of the world since we did away with Diem in Vietnam."

Boyce shuddered at the thought of that action, which had led to the fiasco of the Vietnamese War. The U.S. government had never admitted complicity in Diem's death, but White just had. White looked at him sternly. "Don't you get cold feet on me. You could queer this but good." He waited, but Boyce did not respond. "Well, are you going to tell me?"

"Tell you?"

"Where he's gonna plant the damn tree."

"It's on Kwok-san. Do you know it?"

"Yes. Big place. Anything more definite?"

"Near a village named... Wee-ben."

"Wee-ban," White corrected him.

"Maybe."

"For sure."

14

mission accomplished

Boyce began to wonder whether he would ever have another full night's sleep. He found this one as jumpy and unsatisfying as the last three or four, and he finally rose from his bed as exhausted as he had dropped into it. He found the energy to dress and have breakfast only through the anticipation of what he was about to see on the distant mountain on this fateful day.

He had never thought, in his wildest imagination, that he would be part of a plot to assassinate anyone, let alone a head of state. He could justify it only because he hoped it would lead to Jiwan's liberation. He would do virtually anything to set her free to live a full life. He thought of being put on a plane with her in the middle of the night and flying off to a distant place where under new names they could spend their remaining years together.

Boyce told the hotel desk clerk that he would be gone for most of the day and went out to wait at the curb. He looked for the man with the scar but didn't see him. At precisely 9:00 another of the large black limousines with the darkly tinted windows pulled up. Its driver, different from the one the day before, jumped out and opened the back door for him, and he got in. There, dressed in hiking pants and boots and a pullover leather coat, sat Miss Yi. She reached over and kissed him on the cheek and whispered that she was immensely happy to see him, happy that he had come. Then as the driver got into the front seat she slid back away from him and engaged in light banter. Boyce was once again amazed at her agility and her versatility. She could go in and out of character in a blink of an eye.

Boyce noticed after a few blocks that their car was following an identical black limousine and that another was following them. The procession made its way through the dense traffic, keeping together, and after a long time was moving at an accelerated speed along an open highway. At a certain point the convoy turned onto a secondary road, and after another time they all turned onto a dirt path, all the time climbing higher and higher on a hill side and stirring up an inordinate amount of dust.

The cars continued their climb until they came to a tiny village and pulled to a stop at one of the houses. A peasant woman stood waiting for them, holding a sapling with its roots in a wrapped ball in her right hand. The third car burst open, and six armed guards came rushing out. They stood at attention while Boyce's driver came around and opened the back doors for him and Miss Yi to emerge. They accompanied Boyce and Miss Yi to the first car and watched on high alert as its driver opened the front passenger door and then the two back doors to emit two powerful looking officials, a photographer who looked like the one Boyce had seen at the presidential office, and then the president. Yi got out and stood flexing his muscles, as if the ride had made them stiff. He looked all around, at the hillside, at the village, at the peasant woman coming shyly toward him with the sapling. He noticed his daughter and Boyce and gave them a wave and a smile. They both waved and returned the smile.

"Well, sweet sister," Yi said to the peasant woman. "You have brought me a gift, I see."

The peasant woman smiled, lowered her eyes, and bowed. She stepped forward and offered the sapling to the president. A guard hastily came forward and took the small tree from her and held it for the president.

"Thank you, sister," Yi said to the woman. "You have made a great contribution to the health and prosperity of our nation. I shall plant this tree as a symbol of our efforts to make this indeed once again a green and lush land, a land free of strife, a Garden of Eden for our people."

Yi took the peasant woman's arm and walked up a slope to a spot where a hole had been dug for the tree. When he arrived at the place, the guard brought the tree and set it down by the hole. Another guard produced a shovel. The photographer took a place where he could get the best angle and where the light would be right. It was all a charade, Boyce knew, because the camera held bullets and not film.

Out of the corner of his eye Boyce saw movement, and when he looked he saw another group of men approaching. They were also armed, yet Yi's guards seemed not concerned about them. They were apparently a part of the assemblage, although they had not come with the entourage. Then he heard Yi calling: "Professor Mann, Professor Mann." Yi was looking at him. "You come too.

You should be in the picture, along with this dear sister. Come on."

Boyce hesitated, knowing the danger, but he could not refuse to go and stand by Yi, he could not show fear for his safety, without giving away the plot. He could not disobey the president without causing friction, and the plot had to go smoothly. As he came to the two people ready to have their pictures made, the tree, and the hole where the tree would go, he got his first good look at the new arrivals. Among them was the man with the shock of hair and the scar on his face—and Wright White. He froze. Something was terribly, terribly wrong. The man with the scar was supposed to be one of Ji-wan's people. Wright White was supposed to be with the U.S. mission in Seoul. Neither was supposed to be here in this place at this time.

"Please, Professor, you come stand on this side of me, and sister, you stand here on this side," Yi said. The two of them obeyed. Boyce stood on the president's left and the peasant woman stood on his right.

The photographer asked if they were ready, and the three of them nodded. He aimed and clicked. Boyce flinched, waiting to hear gunfire, waiting for the president to fall and the chaos that was bound to result. Nothing happened. The photographer smiled and said he would repeat, just in case the first picture did not come out. Yi nodded. He clicked again.

Boyce was in a state of shock. The camera was a camera, the photographer was a photographer, the one he had seen at the president's office. He was actually taking pictures. There were no bullets, there was no twin, there was no assassination. Something was wrong, dreadfully wrong.

Then a shot rang out, and the photographer's knees buckled, his camera flew away from him, and he fell toward the hole. Two more shots rang out, and the two guards standing closest to Yi fell, blood spurting from their shirts. Then a barrage of shots, and Boyce felt bullets hitting him in the chest. He fell to his knees, and a calm and cool Yi and a terrified old woman backed away from him. The old woman began to scream, and Yi put his arm around her. Boyce grabbed the sapling and held on to it to steady himself, but the pain was too great, and he let go of it and fell to the ground on his back.

He lay in the fresh grass, still damp from the morning dew. The only sound came from the peasant woman, whose screams of terror had turned to groans of despair. There was no more firing, no one rushing around, only the slow movements of men who had completed a job set for them. They surrounded the two dead guards and the dying photographer.

Boyce knew he was going to die. He tried to speak, but his tongue and throat would not respond, and he could not make a sound. He saw only faces as people gathered around and looked down on him. The man with the scar showed no emotion. He was supposed to be one of Ji-wan's people, but he stood by as bullets tore into four men, including the man who had conspired to assassinate the president and free Ji-wan. He was not who he claimed to be. President Yi and his daughter stood expressionless, showing neither alarm nor regret. They had both known what was about to happen, had sanctioned it, had probably planned it, and despite their claims of friendship, of love, they found in Boyce's death only mild curiosity. Wright White stood, arms crossed over his chest, with a confident smile. Mission accomplished.

Boyce began to see, to understand. The wrong people were dying, or so it seemed to him, according to the plan he had been asked to support, yet everyone seemed satisfied, those who were not supposed to know about the plan, those who said the plan would followed a totally opposite pathway.

Boyce felt his chest tighten. He gasped for breath but none came. He sighed deeply and fell into oblivion.

That night all regularly scheduled programs were dropped from all three Korean television channels. Screens went black, and a deep male voice told the nation to await an address from the president. After a moment of silence, during which millions of viewers waited in nervous anticipation, cameras opened on a live picture of President Yi sitting at a desk.

"Fellow countrymen, I come to you tonight with a heavy heart," he said in a slow cadence, with an expression of sadness on his face.

Around the country Koreans held their breaths. For a quarter century they had been trained to expect and be prepared for an invasion from the North; and many thought this was going to be the president's announcement.

Yi knew this, and he made sure that he began with a note of confidence. "I must first assure you that because of our well equipped and trained armed forces we are secure from outside attack. There is no sign of movement from our common enemy and the millions of our brothers who are held in slavery to his oppressive rule. Communism will never win over us, so long as I am alive."

Around the country there was a collective sigh of relief. There had been no invasion. There would be no bombing, no war, not now at least. Something else was wrong, but at least the people did not have to prepare for a conflict that would surely be even more bloody than the one a lifetime ago.

"I also want to assure you that I am well and in no danger."

Good. The president, the people's bulwark against Northern aggression and enslavement to a godless ideology, was well.

"But I must be forthright, I must be frank and honest with you, I must tell you that this morning there was another attempt on my life, another attempt to thwart the progress of our democracy."

Around the country thousands of faces showed pain in response to the knowledge that another person or persons had tried to kill their leader.

"It was not successful."

People passing apartment buildings walking down streets heard a collective outburst of applause.

"We knew in advance of the attack, we thwarted it."

More applause.

"Here are the facts. I went, as is my custom on this day each year, to plant a tree and thereby encourage our people to return this land to its pristine purity. I went to a much loved site on one of our mighty mountains and accepted the gift of a baby tree from one of our women, herself a national treasure."

On the screen came a picture of the peasant woman holding the sampling aloft. It had to have been taken after the shooting because no photographs were taken before it. The picture was followed by one of the woman handing the tree to Yi, that one also taken after the shooting. In both pictures the woman looked to be in shock, but in the second Yi was smiling.

"I had just accepted the gift and was about to plant the tree in the ground when a shot rang out. Enemies of our democracy had corrupted the man I trusted as my photographer, and instead of a camera he had a gun. He got off several rounds, killing two of my guards before other guards gunned him down."

A picture appeared on the screen, the photographer Boyce had seen at the president's office and the one apparently at the scene of the shooting. Yi made no mention of a twin or a substitute.

"He is a shame to his family, this man, and his name will live in infamy from this time forward. Whereas the two guards who died will receive the highest posthumous award our nations gives—and will be buried in hallowed ground in our cemetery for fallen heroes."

Yi stopped his narrative and cleared his throat. People watching their sets around the country waited.

"The reason I was not injured was to a great extent the work of a man who will live as a hero to this country through time unending. You will know his name, and you will not be surprised when I tell you what he did, for me, for our country. His name is Boyce Mann."

Around the country people nodded and began to cry as a photograph of Boyce flashed on the screen.

"This man, the son of Presbyterian missionaries, the grandson of the first Presbyterian missionaries, this American university professor, today saved my life—and the life of our republic. He stepped in the line of fire and took bullets aimed at me. He died for me, he died for our country."

On the screen came, in succession, photos of the first Boyce Mann and his wife, then the second Boyce Mann and his wife, then of Boyce and his brother Andrew as boys standing in front of the Great South Gate to the city.

"His family has served Korea, has sacrificed themselves for us, since the year 1885, ninety years now. Now another in that line of brave Christian souls has risen to sacrifice himself for us."

Around the country men as well as women and children wiped tears from their faces.

"I have proclaimed this coming Sunday as a Day of National Mourning and Appreciation for Boyce Mann."

Then a series of photographs of the foreigners' cemetery: a long shot of the Mann graves, a close up of the stones of Boyce's grandparents, a close up of the stones of his parents.

"On Sunday he shall be buried with his family in one of our most sacred places, the cemetery where so many foreigners who loved Korea are buried: Missionary Ridge. He will receive the highest honors his church and the state can bestow. Korea will never forget you, Boyce Mann. So long as this nation shall live your name will stand as a beacon of hope in times of trial, as a symbol of all that is best in the American spirit, indeed in the Korean spirit as well. Our two countries will always be friends and allies, comrades in arms, because of the courage and heroism of Boyce Mann on this day."

The camera pulled back from Yi's face to show standing on his left the United States Ambassador to South Korea and on his right his daughter, the First Lady of Korea. Martial music began to play.

Andrew Mann returned to the Missionary Ridge late on Sunday afternoon, three hours after the burial ceremony for his brother. He did not understand what had happened. He got through the services at the church and at the cemetery by blanking out what was going on and letting others guide him to do the proper things. He had spent the next hours drinking.

He walked to the tombstones that told his family history. To the side of his grandparents was the troubled earth of a new grave, without a marker. There just a few hours earlier he had seen his brother's coffin being lowered into the black loam. Boyce was his only real relative, and Andrew knew he would be the last of the Manns. He had no prospects, no desire to find a wife; and if he found one she would of necessity be Korean, a taboo in the family for ninety years. No, he would be obedient, he would shun the shame.

Yet he knew he was a shame himself. He had inherited none of the family gifts. He was not religious, he had no vocation, he was not smart or handsome. He was the one doomed from birth to fail. And fail he had, yes fail he had.

Andrew sat down beside the troubled dirt, put arms around his knees, put his head on one arm, and began to cry. He would live on, if he could call it living, but he had lost his chance to add to the luster of the name. He was not worthy to be called a Mann. He had spent his entire life in Korea, and his brother had been away for 28 years, yet Boyce had returned and within a week died gloriously, heroically, gone out in a blaze of glory, and would always be remembered as the greatest of the great. Andrew would be remembered, if he were remembered at all, as the younger brother who drank himself to death.

Dew was forming on the grass, and Andrew could feel moisture spreading from his hips toward his knees. He could feel his tears spreading from his arm to his chest. He felt like he was drowning. With a moan he stood up and began running, through the tombstones, to the Iron Gate, out into the city. He wanted to lose himself in Seoul.

"He who loses his life shall find it," he said over and over as he ran. "I'll lose mine, I'll lose it, and I'll find it." He had no idea how he would do this, but he knew he must try.

He ran on and on and on.

about the author

T homas Wood, a Peace Corps volunteer who specialized in hydraulic engineering, who now works for a prominent American company, took careful notes on the things he heard and saw while he worked in the R.O.K, from 1974–7. Mission to Seoul is his first novel. The book features barely disguised characters participating in thinly veiled events, captures the essence of those days. Boyce Mann's journey back to the land of his birth, what he finds there, what happens to him there, represent a fiction that Thomas Wood calls "historical fantasy." His story may not have happened, but it did happen.

www.ingramcontent.com/pod-product-compliance
Lightning Source LLC
Chambersburg PA
CBHW070552180626
46817CB00005B/1799